Email

Date: 18th March 2017, 21:21

To: Gary McD,Sammy K, Mark O

Subject: Long time no see….!

Ok, I know it's been a while, but I'm getting married (again!) and was wondering if any of you guys would be up for a bit of a Stag party?

Just the four of us and I'll come back home for a long weekend if you're all up for it.

Mickey O'C

Email

Date: 18th March 2017, 22:10

To: all

Re: Long time no see.

Great to hear from you man! I'm up for it.

When are you thinking of coming over? Do you want me to pick you up at the airport?

Gary

Email

Date: 19th March 13: 23

To: all

Re: Long time no see

Fuck off! Why would I want to meet up again with you bunch of twats

Sgt Sam Kinsale

Email

Date: 24th March 11:00

To: all

Re: long time no see

Good to see we're all still best buddies then!

I wasn't going to bother replying but seeing as old huffy knickers is kicking up a fuss, I think this might be fun.

What dates are you considering? I'll need to book a flight asap.

And don't worry about Sammy, I'll have a word with him and make sure he puts in an appearance.

Mark

Friday 16th June 0830

I had hoped they would all agree to my suggestion of a weekend piss up in the old homeland, but at first it had looked like only Gary was keen on the idea. It took Mark a full week to reply and of course as usual, Sammy was only agreeable if Mark had a word and encouraged or persuaded him to change his mind.

Mark had always been good at changing Sammy's mind. Maybe poor Sam didn't have much of a mind of his own to begin with, or perhaps Mark was just more clever and also sufficiently capable of convincing Sammy that he wasn't being manipulated and that he really did have a mind of his own Even when it had never been true.

In the end, we agreed on the third weekend in June. It suited me for many reasons. I could easily re-arrange my work commitments and find time away from the practice, also it was far enough away from the actual wedding date in July, to be safe should any disasters get in the way. But really it was Mark who decided on the dates. He said it was a good weekend for cheap flights from Spain. As if he needed to worry about the price of a flight. He also said that it had taken a bit of negotiation and compromise to get Sammy to commit to any dates at all. Gary was flexible and said he would make himself available for whatever and whenever we eventually agreed on.

So here we were, back in Northern Ireland, the four of us together after all these years.

Or we would be, whenever the plane eventually made its way into land at, the inappropriately named, Belfast International Airport. The flight had been delayed in Edinburgh due to some storm making its way in from the North Atlantic and causing havoc in both Northern Ireland and Scotland. I think they had named this one, Storm Arlene, which seemed appropriate enough, given the political turmoil filling the headlines on the BBC news website. I had lost all interest in Northern Ireland politics since I had left Queens University in Belfast after graduation in 1983. But I thought it best to catch up with the latest developments in the never-ending story of the Norther Ireland Peace Process, as the country tried again to recover from the latest bitter election. I spent some time in the airport, on my iPad, reading as much as I could be bothered to absorb, but feeling that nothing seemed to have changed at all since I had left.

I had left Northern Ireland because I saw no future for myself there, if I stayed. I figured it was a messy tribal war that would go on forever or at least until a generation evolved far enough removed from the conflict of 1969 to 1991. What we from Northern Ireland called 'the Troubles'. We might as well have described it as a 'wee spot of bother', for all the significance it had been to the rest of the world. Our politicians had led us to believe that 'the Troubles' were over when they signed the Good Friday Agreement in 1998 and so the rest of the world moved on to the next global crisis. These days it seemed to be the threat from ISIS. Ireland's problems were old news now, a page from the history books, for most. Unless you were still living there and hadn't yet come to terms with what was now called the Legacy of the Conflict.

I was getting bored with my planned reading material and my internet browsing was now teasing me away from counter claims of sectarianism to the promotional claims of German car manufacturers. I like my cars and it was time for a change again. One of those new Audi Q7s would be very nice sitting in the underground carpark of my Edinburgh flat.

Friday 16th June 9.00

Belfast International Airport looked different. But not for the better. I suppose I should have expected some change since my last time in the arrivals area, almost 18 years ago. I suspect they will have finally traced my luggage by now. That was the last time I ever saw those golf clubs, but travel insurance is a wonderful thing.

The security regime seemed to have been eased. There was still a tiny sad little lectern at the end of the corridor which made do as a security desk before entering the baggage collection area, but no sign of the two burly police officers who would normally have stood there, eyeing you up and down as if they knew what a terrorist would look like and consequently then be able to arrest them immediately on entry. What did they expect a terrorist to do as he arrived in post ceasefire Belfast? Maybe the post-modernist terrorist would be wearing a T-shirt emblazoned with the slogan 'tiocfaidh ar la' or possibly an old school tie from the Long Kesh Academy. No, the eagle eyes of our homeland security had gone and me and every other passenger on the 9.20 EasyJet flight from Edinburgh, trundled onwards with their hand luggage and barely a glance back at the sparse carousel. For a moment, I thought I saw a set of golf clubs just dipping in under the black rubber strips at the end of the conveyor belt. Probably just wishful thinking and anyway I've given up golf now.

I was hoping that I'd have enough time for a cup of coffee before Gary arrived to pick me up. I'd deliberately lied to him about my flight in the hope that I would have a few minutes to myself just to re-absorb the delights of the place. Eighteen years is a long time and even the air tasted differently. On the other hand, the coffee was still shite and I was just starting to regret paying the £3.40 for lukewarm brown soup pretending to be an Americano, (a decaf version wasn't available), when I heard that voice.

"What about ye big lad!"

I'd know that voice anywhere, full of the countryside with a tinge of city posh. I scanned the arrivals area widely enough to catch sight of the beaming face of our Gary. Still as skinny as ever, but what was left of his hair, had gone grey at the temples. He looked tidy though for his age, a black padded jacket covered a pale blue T-shirt, while dark denim jeans tried to suck up the obligatory black brogues. Black brogues were Gary's default fashion statement, which he'd worn religiously since our school days. He had even refused to move with the times and upgrade to a pair of Dr Martin boots, when the rest of us started wearing that new badge of allegiance to whatever tribe we claimed to be part of. He argued that the boots were a bit thuggish and too quiet. We counter claimed that this was the whole point of them.

He threw his arms around me and I reciprocated. A hug! We didn't used to do hugs. This new post conflict Ireland had clearly gone a bit too far, for my liking. Since I wasn't an experienced hugger, I wasn't sure how long this was supposed to last. I thought it best to leave the timing up to Gary, but already I was feeling uncomfortable that it was going on too long.

"Okay! Okay! You can let go now, I'm not going anywhere."

"You've said that before and I've missed you. It's great to see you again Mickey. Just great!"

He reached down to pick up my case, for a moment I thought he was going to take my hand, as he guided me towards the exit. We passed the loitering taxi drivers, clearly confident of their expected takings for the day, given that this particular International Airport still didn't have a train service and only a 'regular' bus service. For a long time, taxi drivers in Northern Ireland had enjoyed a privileged position in the community. Hopefully a monopoly on airport transfers was the last remnants of that dubious privilege.

"Wait a minute, I've not finished my coffee."

"Don't worry about that, we'll get one down the road. Surely you remembered that the coffee in the airport is pish."

Friday 16th June 09.30

The roads were instantly familiar. I immediately recognised where I was and knew the route we were taking. North towards my old hometown of Ballymena. To the 'Buckle on the Bible belt', where your religion and how much land you owned defined your standing in the community, and the best combination on those two fronts was to be a protestant with a large farm. I might have been brought up a protestant, but my family were never fortunate enough to be able to live off European subsidies, I was more a Council Housing estate kind of boy. Aspiring lower middles class, placing all our bets on the potential riches a good education might one day buy.

How can you love somewhere so much for all that it gave you and at the same time hate it for all that it denied you. It was the 'sense of place' that was bringing us all together now. I knew these guys because we all grew up together in the same town. We lived through Northern Ireland's recent history wearing the same colours and speaking the same words. We sang the same songs and read the same books. We were from the same tribe.

The hedges guided our route and Gary didn't drive fast enough to be at any risk of tossing us into the greenery beyond. He didn't seem to be concentrating on his driving any more than his conversation. We hard hardly spoken since we got into the car. Maybe he had felt he'd gone far enough with the hug.

"I see you are still keeping her between the hedges, man. Nice car by the way, have you had it long?"

"It's an Audi A3, I change it every other year. I like the Audi A4, but Angela says we can't afford one. I'm happy enough with this though. Almost 40 miles to the gallon. Not bad eh! And it's got electrically heated seats."

I hated Audi's and tended to think that they are only bought by people who can't afford BMWs. And why do they all have to be silver?

"Nice colour don't you think? It doesn't show the dirt too much. Although I get it washed every weekend"

"Yeah. Very nice."

We were still driving along the country roads and there was no sign of the of the big dual carriageway that I remembered as the direct route from the Airport to Ballymena. It was the direct and traditional route which would have made for a faster journey, but it was beginning to look as if Gary had other ideas. Unless my memory was a lot worse than I had thought, we weren't even going in the right direction. The efficient clicking of the Audi's indicators warned me of our imminent arrival. It was the entrance to a hotel and one that looked as if it had received a recent make over. As well as some rebranding.

"We can stop off here and get a coffee or something. Are you okay with that?"

"Yeah, fine with me. I don't recognise this place, has it always been here?"

"Yeah, it's a Hilton now, but it used to be called something else. I can't remember what it was before but it's handy and we can catch up over coffee before heading back to the airport."

"Well I was thinking of staying a bit longer than that before catching a return flight."

"No. We're going to pick up Mark as well. His flight isn't due in until 12:20"

The carpark didn't suggest that the hotel was very busy. I didn't know if that was a reflection of the overall economy or just of this hotel. The building looked more like a golf club to be honest and there were enough trolleys and exotically coloured trousers milling around to confirm that it was in fact adjacent to some highly manicured expanses of grass. The sign by the door confirmed it. The Hilton Templepatrick Golf and Country Club. I don't think I had ever walked into anything called a Golf and Country club with any of my old mates, when we were younger, Especially not Gary. We might have hung around outside a few Social Clubs in our day. We maybe even went into the occasional youth club if it was too cold to be loitering outside, but the smell of cigarette smoke or cheap alcohol usually meant our welcome was short lived. I never saw us as Golf club kind of people.

Gary nodded in recognition in the direction of the hotel staff on the reception desk and strode with some confidence into the lounge bar area. A young woman was beside us before we had enough time to drop our coats over the back of the two big leather chairs, that we had decided would be our camp for the rest of the morning.

"Two coffees, please. And I'll have a scone. Do you want one too Mickey, the scones are good in here, especially the wheaten scones."

"I take it, you are a regular in here. Yes. Thanks love, I'll take a scone too."

The waitress left to gather the ingredients for our genteel morning tea. Now as we sat opposite each other, I had time to study Gary more fully since the furtive hugging session. He was older. Around the eyes more creases than wrinkles and the neck was not as firm but stretched by years of shaving with blades that should have been treated as disposable like they were described on the packet. I thought I remembered him as a glasses wearer, but it now looked as if he hadn't been to Specsavers for quite a while. He appeared quite slim, but fortunately for him that came quite naturally. He had always been a skinny wee runt and unlike me he didn't have to depend on the seemingly endless drudgery of the gym treadmill to keep his body fat under control.

"How are you keeping? You look well."

"Thanks. I was just about to say the same to you"

"I used to spend a lot of time on the treadmill. In fact, I still do, but just not to the same extent. I had a bit of a scare a few years ago and I have to keep an eye on my cardio."

"Your what?"

"My heart! I have an irregular heartbeat. It's called Cardio Arrhythmia. It hasn't quite killed me yet, but it could do, if it happens a few more times. I still try to keep fit but I just have to be careful".

"Oh shit man, that's a bugger. Do you have to take tablets for it? Does it affect you in any other way?"

"Like what?"

"Oh, you know."

"No, I don't."

The coffee and scones arrived, and it allowed Gary his obvious enjoyment of admiring the young waitress's gaping blouse. It was good that he had stopped wearing glasses as If he had been wearing them, they would have ended up falling into her bra. Maybe it had happened before and that had led him to consider contact lenses.

The coffee was okay, but the scones were good. I had forgotten how good home baked scones were. Much better than the ones widely available in Scotland. Maybe I was just imagining that. I can't really speak for every scone maker in Scotland. It was only a scone after all, but it did remind me of home and my Granny's baking. Gary did most of the talking while I tried to answer all his questions between mouthfuls of scone. He wanted to know all about my family and my job and at the same time, he wanted to tell me everything about his family and his job. I thought I heard an American voice in my head saying "Previously on Homeland".

Eventually we finished the coffee, the scones and the life story updates. I decided to pay our bill at the reception desk and avoid any further risk to Gary's eyesight or the waitress's dignity.

Friday 16th June 12.30

The electronic arrivals board indicated that a plane from Malaga, Spain had just landed. We made our way to the exit doors from the baggage collection hall. He wasn't hard to spot. Not because we recognised him or saw a figure that we remembered from our past, but because he stood out as the only person in sunglasses, a straw trilby hat and cowboy boots with three-inch Cuban heels.

"All that's missing is the stuffed donkey under his arm. Did he ever grow up and stop acting the idiot?"

"We'll know soon enough. We'll have to wait here until he gets his bag."

There was no response from Gary which made me turn to check if he had heard me. He had also turned around and was looking in the direction of the entrance doors, as a swaggering loutish figure strutted towards us

"What the fuck are you two doing here? I thought I wouldn't be seeing you until later when we reached the hotel in Ballymena. Is the dickhead's flight in yet?"

"Who are you calling a dickhead!"

Gary took off, like a cross breed dog let off the leash. He had barely covered half the distance between himself and Sammy, before throwing himself full force into his target's chest. But Sammy was ready for him and pretending to find it amusing, he created a fleeting impression of an ulster bullfighter and turned his body sideways to allow Gary to crash to the floor without making the contact he had intended.

Sammy glared at me and held his hands out wide and shrugged "What the fuck was that about, What did I do …?."

But Gary was already scrambling to his knees and rugby tackled his foe from behind pushing him forward onto his face, which made a loud slap as it connected with the tiled flooring of the International Airport's arrival lounge. This ensured that everyone who hadn't already noticed the unusual fracas, was now fully alerted to the sight of two men trying to pull themselves to their feet while at the same time pushing the other one back onto the floor. Sammy was bleeding from the side of his mouth as a result of his face plant while Gary was wearing a small trickle of blood from his nose. It appeared that Gary still had the upper hand of the attack and began the second phase of the offense line with another wild push into Sammy's chest. Sammy went backwards and let go of the paper bag he had been holding since the skirmish started. The bag ripped causing four strange shallow cone shaped buns to roll around in circles at his feet.

"Ah fuck, not the Paris buns. I bought one for each of us. Wise up you wee shite."

Gary followed up his shove to the chest with a wildly inaccurate kick. It missed Sammy but he managed to grab hold of the attached black brogue shoe and pulled its owner off balance and down heavily onto his back. Now with both sprawled horizontally, it looked like a Greco Roman wrestling match was inevitable, until Sammy began to squeal under the pressure of a well shone cowboy boot on his upper arm and Gary was similarly disabled under the weight of a large orange trolley case pressing forcefully on his chest.

"That's enough ladies! I know you're both delighted to see me, but there is no need to grovel".

Mark had arrived on the scene and taken advantage of both his vertical position and his recently reclaimed luggage. "Mickey give me a hand here! You hold Gary and I'll deal with Sammy."

I obliged, helping Gary to his feet and took a firm restraining grip of his arm. I was conscious that the trickle of blood from his nose was gaining some momentum and I hadn't packed enough shirts to be letting this one become an early blood splattered casualty. Gary looked as if he was about to cry with frustration or maybe it was just an interaction with a dusty floor and a contact lens dependent fifty something face. His breathing was fast and shallow, I could feel his chest heave and fall, but he didn't try to pull away from my grip. I got the impression that he was waiting for something else to happen.

Just a couple of feet away. Mark stood with his back to us like an inappropriately dressed NFL line-backer blocking the agitated but rapidly calming Sammy. He was dusting himself down and had already found a tissue to tend to his bleeding mouth. He didn't appear to be as expectant as Gary and I got the impression that the fight was over as far as he was concerned. I wasn't sure if that was down to the presence of Mark or by his own choice.

The attendant crowd were trying to look disinterested but maintained their ground for the sake of a good view. They had formed an elongated circle around us, some clutching their trolleys and others shielding young kids from the sight of the nasty men. Two security guards had emerged from the background and were making their way through the women with children, assorted wagons and trolleys. If security are supposed to exude an impression of authority, these two had already failed. Their most threatening feature was the size of their beer bellies and the fear that eventually it would be the death of both of them. Otherwise, they just oozed authority. And sweat.

"Before you ask, there's nothing wrong. Everything here is ok. He's just not a big fan of Paris buns." said Mark kicking the last spiralling pastry in the direction of the security guard.

"It didn't look like that on the CCTV. Are you gentlemen ready to leave now or do we need to take this further."

"I'm more than happy to take it further" grunted Gary as he managed to pull away from my grip and launch himself at Sammy again. But his initial thrust planted his brogues firmly on one of the Paris buns, squishing it and causing it and him to slide sideways. Completely unbalanced, he fell into the grasp of the other Security Guard.

"Aw, Gary, I didn't recognise you there. It's me Billy from the lodge. Are you ok mate? Is this guy annoying you?"

Gary pulled himself immediately to attention, which allowed him to recognise one of his fellow Orangemen from the local Loyal Orders. I assumed it was the same Orange Lodge, although it might have been the Masonic Lodge they were talking about, but either way it was enough for Gary to assume a more respectable demeanour and assure his new knight in shining armour that all was in order. We were all friends and we'd be on our way forthwith.

I followed behind Gary towards the automatic glass doors and Mark held back a few feet, chatting to Sammy but soon heading in the same direction. We all pulled up together at the kerb waiting for a break in the traffic stuttering through the Drop off zone.

"So where are we parked?" smirked Marc.

In the same breath both Gary and Sammy announced, "Over there" and pointed in opposite directions of the Short Stay Car park.

"That's nice! You decided to give me a choice then, or did you just not think to talk to each other and make some practical arrangements about this big weekend".

Mark followed Sammy in one direction, while Gary and I headed in the other back to the Audi. It was starting to rain. Not heavily but just enough to make you feel miserable. And wet.

"Whose idea was it to ask him to turn up at the airport?"

"I'm guessing Mark did. But I don't know why, unless they had something they needed to talk about. Or maybe he just doesn't like your driving skills."

"I agreed that I would do the necessary airport pick-ups and then he could join us when we got to the Hotel".

"D'ya mean in Ballymena or Belfast?"

"I'd prefer if I never saw him again anywhere, but you wanted all four of us to get together for this weekend, so I thought I could control myself. For you. But ...."

"You need to get over that you know. Do you still think that he was shagging Angela while you were working nights in Portrush?"

"She denies it, and so does he. But he always had a smug look on his face if we ever met and she hates the idea of me speaking to him. I doubt if I'll ever know for sure, but I just can't shift the idea from my mind. I remember once, when we were not long married, arriving home early from work one day. I walked in and there they were. Him and her sitting in our living room. All calm and collected. It was weird. Not even a cup of tea or coffee between them. They claimed he had called round to talk to her about an incident at her work. It was when he was based in the local police station. Looking back on it now, I was a bit of a fool for accepting such a weak explanation, but I let it go at the time and there seems no point in going back over it now. I've heard a few other things from other friends but not enough for a 'conviction', so to speak. Anyway, if I want our marriage to work, I just have to suck it up. But I don't have to like it."

"You're best not to think about it too much. Sure, he was always a bit of a dick anyway. Did you see that he still signs his emails, Sgt Sam Kinsale. He's been out of the force for years, hasn't he?"

"Yeah, ever since they changed their name from the RUC to the PSNI and offered early redundancy to all the old psychopaths who were too fat or too bitter."

A silver Mercedes had pulled up behind us in the queue to exit through the barrier of the airport short stay car park. The Mercedes flashed its headlights and turning around to check out what was up, I could see Mark's broad grin and two fingers gesturing at us. Sammy however wasn't smiling at all and seemed more interested in checking out for any damage to his teeth in the rear-view mirror.

"I think you might have knocked out one of his teeth back there. He's still poking his finger in his mouth and I don't think it has stopped bleeding yet."

"Hey ho! An eye for an eye and a tooth for a tooth! As they say."

Friday 16th June 13.00

"I'm not sure breaking his tooth adequately balances out your wife's affair with a lunatic. But I know what you mean."

We drove in convoy for the rest of the journey. Gary driving the Audi and Sammy driving the Mercedes, at a less than safe distance behind. It was ok while we were negotiating the smaller roads around the town of Antrim but once we got onto the faster dual carriageway, I'm sure it would have been better if the other two didn't join us in the back seat just yet. Gary was obviously feeling the strain as well and started to mess around by stabbing on the brakes and then accelerating. Their little game of cat and mouse, might have been funny when they were teenagers, but as two grown men who had long since graduated from driving their boy racer Vauxhall Novas and were now somehow able to purchase two much more powerful German manufactured vehicles, this had the potential to get dangerous or at best attract the attention of the local traffic police.

"Have you had this Audi long?"

"About a year, I guess. I change it every two years."

"I'd have thought you'd have learnt to drive it a bit better by now".

"Don't you start as well. It's him, he's driving up my arse. He needs to back off with his old man's car."

"If a Merc is an old man's car, what do you call an Audi then?"

"Anyway, Mark would look more at home in a white Mercedes."

Together, we both laughed out, "Drug dealer's car!"

"Do ya think …."

"Don't even go there!"

We were approaching the outskirts of Ballymena. The dual carriageway was about to end in the inevitable roundabout, so Gary started to slow down. Obviously, Sammy had no intention of following him. The Mercedes flashed past on the inside lane. I saw the single finger of the driver raised especially for us followed by brake lights and a screech of expensive rubber. The car wobbled as if it was about to roll over into the central mound of the roundabout, but its bulk and width held it tight to the turn and with just a hint of over steer, managed to get all the way around the roundabout in one piece. I wasn't sure if Gary was impressed or pissed off but his grimace made me think he had been surprised by Sammy's rally style overtaking manoeuvre. By the time we got to the other side of the large stone sign which offered a Welcome to Ballymena, the Mercedes was out of sight.

"Arsehole!" said Gary. "I assume he knows where we are going?"

"Isn't there another way to get to the Hotel without driving through the town?"

"Well remembered, ballbeg. Now, if you could just tone down that little Scottish twinge in your voice, we might start to believe that you did actually grow up in this town."

The traffic was kind to us, clearly Friday afternoons weren't as busy as they used to be. We reached the carpark of the Hotel just in time to see Mark lifting his suitcase from the boot of the Mercedes. Gary choose not to take the available space immediately beside the other two. That was ok with me too but Sammy looked pleased with himself.

So here we were. All four of us, for the first time in many years, standing together in the car park of the Adair Arms hotel. We had been here many times before. Usually standing in a line to get into the disco on a Saturday night or taking a short cut between any one of a number of bars that made up our normal weekend adventures. As I remembered it, Montgomery's bar was around the corner, the Grouse Inn was across the large shopping centre car park, the George was a short walk away and those were only the bars where we might have been considered as regulars. There were plenty of others, for such a god-fearing town, Ballymena was well served by bars. I was looking forward to visiting a few of them over the weekend but as we all stood looking at each other in the small hotel car park, there was more than a hint of apprehension. We each stood ready by our cases, but no one was moving. We just posed there, looking at each other with our arms by our sides, holding our various pieces of luggage as if we were about to pull out guns from the cases and start our own version of the Gunfight at the OK Corral. The town hall clock didn't have a bell but it would have been a good time for it to chime and break the silent stand-off. Instead, it was Mark who broke the silence.

"This feels good. Great memories, eh lads?"

"And a few not so good memories too!" Said Sammy and Gary at the same time, as if they had been rehearsing it.

"Well, I'm really grateful that we've all been able to make it. It means a lot to me to see you all again. And I do know that there is some history which might be better left in the past, but there were plenty of good times too. So, can we call a truce? For this weekend, at least?", I said, trying to look them each directly in the eye as I spoke. I think I got three simultaneous nods of agreement. Well, it was start.

Friday 16th June 13.30

I had chosen the Hotel as it was in the centre of town and was a permanent fixture of our past. It was as if the town had been built around the Adair Arms Hotel. The hotel lobby opened up directly onto the street on what used to be one of the busiest roads in town. The adjacent wide junction was formed by the meeting of five main roads and was known as the Pentagon. Those five roads used to arrive with authority bringing travellers from the many outlying villages which depended on Ballymena as a market hub. But since the town's road system had been restructured by various wise men from the town planning departments of local government and encouraged by a few private developers, those same five roads seemed to have lost their way. They may arrive at the Pentagon but it was no longer quite so obvious where they had come from and it certainly wasn't immediately apparent if they might actually take you anywhere you might want to go.

The old cinema cried out for some tender loving care from the other side of the street opposite the Hotel, the decommissioned courthouse was on one side and the mysterious Masonic Hotel on the other. All the buildings within view looked as if they had been there forever and certainly since the town was at its peak, and a prosperous market town built on the best Presbyterian endeavours of the surrounding farmland.

Ballymena has a lot of churches, at least thirty Presbyterian ones not to mention a few of each of the other main brands. And then there is Green Pastures and its ilk, I told you not to mention them. It's quite a successful franchise, more successful than many other fried food outlets, but not as wholesome. The churches make good money too. From the weekly envelopes to the midweek silent collections. They pull in quite a bit of cash, what do they need all that money for, anyway? Cash too, which is notoriously hard to trace, so the Tax men say. Religion encloses the town like a huge wet blanket. It smells stale and taints everything, you just can't escape it, it spoils everything. They are particularly good at preying on the vulnerable. But the town still has more pubs than churches, though I think the churches make more money and are more likely to stay open longer. How about one last wee prayer before we head home.

If I was to stand at the front door of the hotel, I think I could claim to have been inside every building that I could see, and that included the various solicitor's offices and the court house. I'm sure I must have been inside that Church at some time, but I remembered the inside of the other buildings more vividly.

I wanted to have a good look around to check if my memories were any match for the reality of the place, but we had entered from the rear of the hotel and were headed directly for the reception desk, where Mark and I would check into our rooms. I was surprised when Sammy and Gary headed off on their own to find a seat in the bar area and order up a few pots of coffee.

"How can they act so calm now after that farce at the airport?"

Mark shrugged his shoulders and said, "Home turf, I suppose."

We had two rooms booked and the girl on reception was kind enough to offer to arrange for our bags to be carried up to our rooms if "we wanted to join our colleagues for coffee". I thought she might be mistaking us for someone else, but Mark just smiled his big winning smile back at her and said "Ah yes, Love, our colleagues will be wanting to get down to business as soon as possible, that would be great if you just looked after the cases and get someone to organise some coffee for us."

We soon found the other two sitting in a bay window of the hotel bar area, not wrestling but not chatting much either. "I hope we're not interrupting anything," said Mark, "Do you come here often?"

"Aye right!" replied Sammy, "Coffee is on its way. Sit down, for fuck sake, before anyone sees you."

"I haven't done anything wrong. I'm quite entitled to be here. Unless you have a problem with being seen with me. Or Mark or Gary, for that matter."

Sammy snarled back, "We might all have grown up in this town, and we might all have a past of some sort, but Gary and I still live here, while you tossers just blow in for the weekend with your money and your memories as if it's all just rosy in the garden. I have a reputation in this town, and I'm not sure an ex-cop should be seen huddled over a few cups of posh coffee with a suspected drug dealer."

"Now steady on big boy, I've never been convicted of anything of the sort and I'm pretty sure that Mickey's dental practice doesn't offer anything stronger than a few paracetamols!"

Gary spoke up, "Wind your neck in Sammy. That's so bloody typical of you to over dramatize everything. Anyway, as you said you're an ex-cop now. I doubt if the MI5 code of practice still applies to Shopping Centre Security Senior Administrative Operatives.

I looked at Sammy, inviting him to comment, Mark looked at Gary, as if he had been excluded from the joke . "Well that's what it says on his LinkedIn Profile. I checked him out when we started planning this thing."

"Ok, so that's a fair place to start. Cards on the table, who and what are we all, these days. A quick pen picture over coffee. I'll start."

Coffee arrived followed immediately by another waiter with another tray and another four cups and another large pot.

"Are we expecting company?"

"Fuck up! I ordered at reception and you must have already ordered at the table. It's fine. We'll drink it. I'm up for Mickey's idea. A bit of honesty to start this weekend would be useful to help cut through the bullshit. Go ahead Mickey."

"Ok, I'm Mickey O'Connor, previously of this parish but now living in Edinburgh, Scotland where I have a dental practice. Previously married to Liz, also of this parish. But now I'm about to get married in a months' time to Bernie, not of this parish."

"I'm Gary McDowell, never left this parish I was born in, still married to Angela, with two kids, William and Samantha. I'm a civil servant, working in the Department of Work and Pensions, in Belfast."

"Sam Kinsale. I don't know what this shite talk of parishes is all about, but I was born, bred and buttered in Ballymena and since I took early redundancy from the Police, I've been working in Security for a private firm. Oh, and I'm married, and we have one boy."

Mark stood up, spread his arms as wide as he could and announced, "Let me present, Mark Orr, international playboy and entrepreneur, grew up in this wee shit hole of a town but left when I caught myself on and now live near Malaga. That's in Spain, Sammy. I have sort of retired but still like to keep my hand in. Talking of which I have a wife called Maria, she's never been to Ireland, and I'd prefer to keep it that way."

I knew most of that anyway. We're all on the internet, and none of us had enough wit to adjust our privacy settings on Facebook, but somehow it diffused the tension a bit. We started questioning each other about what we had just heard. How is the wife? How old are the kids? Where's your house? How's work these days? The usual sort of thing and easy chatter over coffee. Non-threatening, non-invasive and vague enough to avoid the feeling of being interrogated. I suspect we had all learnt something new.

The talk started to turn to how the old hometown had changed. I was keen to hear about all our old haunts from our younger days. Inevitably that ended up with both Mark and I firing a stream of questions at Sammy and Gary.

Ballymena was a large town by Northern Ireland standards, maybe over 65,000 of a population, and although a lot smaller than the bigger city of Belfast, just 30 miles south. It was, or had been a wealthy town, although the stories we were now hearing put that in some doubt. It was often known as the 'Buckle on the Bible belt', being a reflection of its very strong protestant church ethos and central location in the rich farmlands of County Antrim. The town had benefitted from its farming hinterland and a number of large factories paying good wages for many years. Although most of its people would have belonged to one or other of the variety of protestant churches, it was a minor irritant to those most holy that many of its more famous names in history, sport and the arts were from the other persuasion. Or 'them'uns' as they were often called.

Gary and Sammy agreed that times were indeed changing. Two of the large local factories had recently closed and the town was struggling to retain its reputation as a 'great place to shop, hey'. Gary seemed sure that the new coffee culture and his extensive list of local coffee shops, would sustain the town's economy for a few years yet. Sammy wasn't just as positive and complained that the town was full of car washes operated by eastern European immigrants. But they both agreed that most of the decent pubs had closed and bemoaned that a town which once boasted 96 bars, could now barely offer a respectable handful, or certainly not enough which old timers like us, would like to be seen in.

"It was always, The Grouse, The Countryman's, The George, Montgomery's, what happened?"

"Well at least three of those still exist. Kind of. But you wouldn't go from pub to pub on a Saturday night, the way we used to. There's a few dodgy places at the top of the town, or a couple of decent bars in the villages but I wouldn't go into them on my own or without the company of a local."

"It was always like that. We would never have ventured into pubs north of Ballymoney Street. The top of the town was enemy territory. It was full of them'uns."

In truth the town did have a bit of a north south split. A bit like an inverted North America, with the rebel estates all in the republican North as opposed to the Deep South, where bars like The Raglan and the Moat bar where were the Union flag flew highest. Although it was often accompanied by a few other flags.

"So, I'm guessing that the plan for the weekend, doesn't include a pub crawl of all the old bars?" asked Mark.

"Well maybe we could visit a few of them when it's still daylight tomorrow, but no I was thinking we could do Belfast tonight, then hit a decent restaurant on the coast tomorrow night," replied Gary.

"Yip, I'm up for that. Maybe tomorrow night we could even try to get into some of the old nightclubs around the Port!"

"Is your head cut. I'm way too old for nightclubs. I'm not looking for that kind of stag party anyway."

"I'm ok with any of that but I don't want to be driving while you twats get to do all the drinking."

"Don't worry Mr Traffic Branch, I'll pay for a taxi. My treat"

"They might still prefer cash, but I doubt if they'll take Euros."

"Touché Turtle! Those were the days; it was amazing what you could get a taxi driver to do for the right amount of cash."

"Enough already! If Mark is offering to pay for a taxi, and Mickey doesn't have a car with him, that would make sense. And you don't have to drive Sammy. Will 'what's her name' allow you out for the night then?"

"Her name is Jenny and yes a taxi would be a great idea, seeing as Loads-a-Money is paying."

It looked like we had managed to form a plan and the excessive coffee consumption was starting to put some pressure on our ageing bladders. I stood up and announced I needed to go to my room. Everyone else got to their feet and seemed equally relived for an excuse to visit the boy's room.

"Let's all do whatever we have to do and meet back here in the hotel bar at 6:00. The receptionist can call us a taxi and we should be in Belfast by 7:00 by the latest."

"Ok back here for six, it is. And everyone suited and booted for the bright city lights of Belfast."

Mark followed me to reception to pick up our respective room keys. I watched Sammy and Gary, continue to talk as they made their way out to their nice posh cars in the carpark. I was glad that they seemed to have set their differences aside and could talk to each other with some civility. Even if it was only about miles per gallon or service intervals. Maybe my original expectations for a last weekend with a few old mates, was going to happen after all.

Friday 16th June 14.30

I had some unpacking to do. Mainly putting shirts onto hangers, in a futile attempt to reduce any need to use the electric smoothing iron supplied by the hotel for the more dapper and domesticated traveller. I also made sure to take each of my tablets. I had promised Bernie, that I'd be careful, but I was only going so far with that promise. I might have lied to her a little about my intentions and terms of engagement with the local beers. Well about the Guinness at least. Most of the other beers were just fizzy dishwater as I remembered them. But Guinness was always better at home or was that just an old myth.

I decided to take a quick shower and brush my teeth. As I towelled myself dry in the marble effect bathroom, I paused in front of the full-length mirror and caught myself considering my naked body for a second or two longer than a man my age should really. It wasn't that I was overweight. I did some running and went to the gym, although maybe not as much as I used to do. But I had hoped to see the young man that I use to be when I lived in this town and he just wasn't there anymore. Coming of Age in Ballymena, meant graduating from the toy pages to the underwear pages of the Kays catalogue. I had never considered myself as getting any older until I had my little health scare a few years back. I still had my hair, or most of it. There were no blurred and darkened tattoos to regret. I'd managed to avoid glasses but only at the expense of laser eye surgery about five years ago. Okay so some of the teeth were 'man made' and the toothpaste I was using was keen to promote it's 'ultra-bright whitening' qualities. I had the remnants of a winter tan that provided some disguise for the wrinkled skin that continued to appear, although uninvited, with every trip to the Mediterranean sunshine. There was no six pack, but I believed I could still see a firm chest and a strong set of shoulders. I could still put my socks on in the morning without wakening anyone up. I was just about to clasp my hands together and flex my triceps muscles, but as I started to turn to my side and raised one knee at an angle, I froze. Then catching myself on, I shuddered with embarrassment and went to the wardrobe to find a nice loose fit striped shirt.

As I continued to get myself 'suited and booted' as per the lads' instructions, I turned on the TV and listened to the local news. I enjoyed hearing the familiar home accent again, even though the presenters were doing their best to read the studio autocue in their best BBC voices. I remembered the old presenters that we had grown up with. Those regular faces that we had watched each evening as they told us of another bomb somewhere or another killing. It became very ordinary to hear of another death from one side or the other. As long as, the name wasn't one you recognised or it had happened in another part of the country that you didn't frequent, then it just became the normal routine. You didn't have to concern yourself with the impact each sectarian murder had on the loved ones left behind. Northern Ireland was never going to change, and no one expected the same blinkered politicians to be able to find, let alone look for, a solution. Living in Ballymena, 'the Troubles' seemed to always happen somewhere else. Mostly Belfast or Derry, sometimes along the border or someplace like Crossmaglen where no one I knew, had ever been. 'The Troubles' for me were something I saw on the TV just like the rest of the world and it was only when I ventured out of our own little Ballymena bubble, that it had any effect on me. But that didn't stop me telling everyone I met that I was from Northern Ireland, where there was a war going on. Except we didn't call it a war we called it 'the Troubles'. Which I suppose reflected the fact that on most days, for me, it was more of a nuisance than a threat to my life.

It wasn't until I went to University in Belfast that my experience of 'the Troubles' changed, and I began to realise that 'the Troubles' posed a threat to my future as much as it posed a threat to a lot of other people's lives. I met a lot of people who had grown up in Derry (that was before I realised that apparently, people like me were supposed to call it Londonderry) and who had experienced a lot of 'the Troubles' in ways other than on TV. Some had seen bombs and shootings. Some had relatives in prison, some had relatives that I thought should have been in prison. One girl I met told me about having to take her bicycle home and hose it down, after she had left it propped up against the wall of a sweet shop when a bomb had exploded nearby. The flesh of a young soldier was sprayed all over her new red bike. Just like me she just got on with it. Cleaned her bike and lived her life. Although I think her life had been very different to mine. But all NI children were raised with a fear of cutlery. The sharp knife and the wooden spoon could strike terror into us all more than any threat of terrorism.

I was sitting on the edge of the bed, staring directly into the TV screen. It was ten to six. I hadn't realised the time passing. I was too busy remembering it.

I stood up, buttoned up my shirt cuffs and swept my hands through my hair. There wasn't really enough hair to warrant the full hand sweep but it made me feel good. A quick splash of aftershave. Nothing too expensive, I didn't want to come across as too flash. I checked my pockets for the necessities, wallet, phone, emergency tablets, tissue. I smiled as I remembered that the list would once have also included a pack of cigarettes, a lighter and a condom. At least some of those changes were for the better. If not all of them.

I got to the bottom of the stairs and smelled him before I could see him.

"That's some aftershave you've got there."

Mark spun round and with one of his usual big grins, replied, "Do ya like it? It's a Harvey Nixx exclusive and bloody expensive."

Friday 16th June 18.00

The taxi arrived on time, just as the hotel receptionist had promised it would. We had told her that we needed a car large enough to take four people and I think the battered old Mercedes C class might just fulfil that need, as long as one of us didn't mind sitting up front with the driver. We let him know we'd be out soon as possible. He was happy to wait, as he savoured his anticipated profit on such an easy straightforward run up to Belfast in the early evening.

Sammy was next to arrive, swaggering into the hotel foyer from the direction of the rear car park. He didn't seem too worried that he was keeping the rest of us waiting but he certainly had given a bit of attention to his appearance. Most notable was his hair or more so the wet look hair gel which seemed to have been applied to his entire head. Including his moustache and eyebrows. As he came closer, I was sure I could even see globules of it around and inside his ears. He was wearing a smart blue linen jacket over a plain white shirt, open at the collar far enough to display a hint of dark chest hair trying to escape and threatening to strangle him. Again, a smart pair of dark jeans drew your eye to the ubiquitous black brogues.

"Looking good kid! Who dressed you?"

As we stood near the doorway, where the taxi driver and each of us could keep an eye on each other, it was impossible to miss the silver Audi driven by a pretty blonde as it pulled up on the opposite side of the street. I wasn't just as disappointed as Mark obviously was, to see, Gary's wee balding head bend forward to plant a kiss on the blonde's cheek before hoping out of the car. He was in the process of lifting his hand to wave her off, when he noticed the three of us staring at him through the Hotel's glass doorway. It looked as though he had intended to blow her a kiss but panicked and with a ninja like hand sweep suddenly turned his movement into a shoulder height karate chop. The blonde spoiled the illusion by continuing with her hand kissed response and a puzzled look at her husband.

Gary didn't come into the hotel but gestured for us to join him as he opened the door of the waiting taxi. I used the revolving glass door to ensure that I was first out and joining Gary in the back seat. Mark similarly realised what was going on and placed a strategic cowboy boot where it made the revolving door shudder and ensure that Sammy would be held back and forced to take the final seat in the taxi. The dreaded front seat.

Once the driver had tidied up his used coffee cups, swept some sausage roll crumbs from the seat and forced his crumpled morning paper into the side panel of his cockpit, Sammy was able to take up his honoured position. He was now the spokesperson for our party and therefore responsible for dealing with all enquiries. We had barely managed to adjust to the overpowering pong of the Greentree air freshener dangling from the rear-view mirror, before Sammy and the driver had commenced the necessary negotiations.

"So where are we going tonight then lads?"

"Belfast City Centre"

"I didn't know there were any protests on at city hall tonight!" he laughed. No one else did.

"So, whereabouts in the city"

Sammy felt sufficiently confident to offer his more recent and superior knowledge of the city's nightlife. "I was thinking of starting at the John Hewitt. Are you guys ok with that?"

"Fine by me!", "Whatever you say, big boy", "Sounds like a good plan".

We were now committed, there was no further need for discussion with the driver, we could leave that up to Sammy. It didn't take long. We hadn't even reached the dual carriageway before we heard him ask the driver "So are you busy tonight?"

We were on our way.

Friday 16th June 18.30

When I was a young boy, trips to Belfast were few and far between. Even before the shooting and bombing had become a common everyday feature, it seemed that our family were able to find everything they needed in Ballymena's shops. And it was a waste of petrol to take whatever dodgy car my Dad had that year, on a day trip to the city. But when we did go, I loved it. I loved the buzz. I loved the buses. I loved the sound of the paper boys shouting 'tele'. Belfast was somehow more important than my wee town and it looked more important. City Hall was magnificent and the shops on Royal Avenue were impressive inside and out.

But by the time I got to live there myself, as a student at Queen's University, it had lost a lot of its intrigue for me. The city centre was like some cheap temporary fortress with security checks at every turn. Shops had security guards who would frisk you without any enthusiasm for their job or your dignity. The windows on the big buildings were criss-crossed with tattered clear sticky tape as a potentially futile attempt to minimise the spread of shattering glass in the event of a car bomb attack. Metal grills covered doorways and battleship grey was the paint colour of choice and the cheapest available for the blocked-up windows. In every way that grey colour was how I remembered Belfast from my student days. It was boring and dirty and unfriendly rather than dangerous.

It took only 35 minutes to pull off the motorway and drop us off as near to the John Hewitt bar as the taxi driver could negotiate. Already I could see the city had changed. It looked like a city and it even had some colour. New shops had replaced the many informal car parks, that proliferated the inner west of the city. I don't think I had ever been in a car near St Anne's Cathedral before. Yes, I had walked past it on a few occasions, but it was in the wrong part of the city for me. A bit like Ballymena and the north of the town, St Anne's represented 'them'uns' territory and the beginning of the notorious West Belfast. But now St Anne's Cathedral represented the new beginning of the modern Belfast. This was the Cathedral Quarter, the new cosmopolitan social hub of Belfast. Like other European cities, Belfast now had a Quarter. A Quarter! Where we used to have a ghetto. Or so said many of the people I knew back then.

Mark was speaking to the taxi driver and hopefully paying him, as he had promised he would. We all stepped out into a mild night, still plenty of bright daylight for a June evening and while not quite the Spanish Costas, it was warm enough to justify Sammy's wife's choice of a linen jacket.

Inside, the bar looked as if it had always been a part of Belfast and that it was where wee men in flat caps had spent all their wages from the Harland and Wolf shipyard. It had character, as the marketing team would have said.

"Did we ever drink in here before? Like when we were younger."

"Nope, never."

"Why not, it looks like somewhere I remember."

"That's because it is supposed to look like that. But we never drank in here because it only opened in 1999".

"No way"

"Yip, way"

I almost felt disappointed that our first stop on this nostalgia pub crawl, wasn't even part of my past.

"So why did we come in here then?"

"For the beer. They do bloody great beers!"

Sammy and Gary were already at the taps, staring at what was on offer from the bewildering range of beers most of which I had never heard of before. I liked my craft ales and lagers, but I just didn't recognise anything.

"I was expecting you and Sammy to be hardened Harp drinkers." I said. "It used to always be a toss up between Harp or Tenants when we went out."

"We're not as backward as you big city slickers from Edinburgh might think. I haven't drunk Tenants in years. I love these wee craft breweries and all those hoppy ales and shit. Why don't you try one" Gary offered.

Sammy was gesturing at a bottle labelled 'Sailor Town Beer" and Gary added a schooner of Hercules, to the instructions for the barman. I looked at Mark, who shrugged his shoulders and asked the barman for a pint of 'Brewdog' Punk. "What the fuck is a schooner, anyway?"

"You've all turned out to be a right bunch of posey buggers. A schooner! Does that come with a little paper umbrella and a sparkler? What's wrong with you guys. I have memories that I want to protect and cherish here. None of this new metropolitan Belfast chic. I'll have a Guinness please. And in a pint glass too."

It was still early for a Friday evening and although there were plenty of the "just one after work" crowd already in the bar, we managed to get a table and hunkered down to try and hear ourselves over the lardle dardle of the Belfast chatter. It was full of the type of people who would have thought Michael Jackson's Moon Walk was more impressive than Neil Armstrong's. I was looking forward to this. Just the four of us, together with a few beers and the night ahead of us to fill with more beers and a bit of banter from the past.

"So what do you think of Belfast then Mickey?", started Gary, taking a first swig of his schooner and adjusting himself with a little shudder of his shoulders, as if he was settling in for the night.

"Aye, do you see many changes?" interrupted Sammy.

"Well, it's not that I've seen much of it yet but yes so far, it isn't how I remember it" I managed to say before Mark took over.

"Listen guys, we are here because Mickey wanted us to help him celebrate his impending marriage to the lovely Bernie. Well, I assume she's lovely, I've never met her. But he wants a few beers, a bit of a laugh and a few stories about the good old days. And definitely nothing about the bad old days. Ok!"

"That sounds like the words of a man who would rather forget his past than have to explain it", I said as I cast a look at the other two, looking for some hint of support."

"No, I was no saint back in the day, but I've already spoken to the other two about this and it makes more sense if we start off the way we mean to go on. The weekend should be about a few lads having some fun, a bit of a laugh, not a fucking public enquiry. Northern Ireland has had enough of those. Am I right guys?"

Sammy seemed eager to grab hold of this new line of conversation immediately and launched into a tirade about the amount of public money he insisted had been wasted on the numerous historical reviews into various atrocities carried out during the troubles. He seemed particularly aggrieved at the Bloody Sunday Enquiry and his voice escalated in volume at a surprising rate. Gary seemed to agree with him for the most part and Mark was happy just to sit back and observe the damage caused by his little verbal grenade. I thought he looked quite happy with what he achieved, as if he was enjoying the wind up.

"Keep your voice down a bit, Sammy. I'm not sure if everyone in this pub would agree with the opinions of an ex-cop from Ballymena about the rights and wrongs of British Army's Parachute Regiment in 1971"

"It was the same in school. When our teacher, Mr Flanagan got us to discuss this one day in RE class, you were the only one who seemed to think that the rioters had a right to be on the streets. Whereas the rest of the class felt that if you don't want to get shot you should be more careful about getting caught up in a riot." Sammy wasn't interested if anyone was listening or prepared to re- evaluate their viewpoints of historical events that might still be pretty raw for those who had maybe more direct experience of that day. He just expected his three mates to agree with him and for anyone else in the vicinity to mind their own business. But even in a busy bar, Sammy's Ballymena accent was coming to the boil and I could see a few heads turn to look in our direction. There was no sense of threat, but Mark looked at me and I knew that we both felt it was time to be going.

"Fair enough Sammy, but as Mark has already said, before you went off on one. This weekend shouldn't be about the bad old days, should it?"

Gary stood up and took a long final slug of his Belfast beer, Sammy hesitated but quickly relented and downed the end of his bottle. Mark was already making his way to the door while I held my arm out like a protective parent, waiting to guide Sammy and Gary away from the scary starey people.

"What was all that about?" Sammy wasn't happy and neither was Mark. As he pulled Sammy to one side, I heard Mark start to say "Look I've told you to tone this down a bit ...." before his instructions in Sammy's ear turned to a whisper. Gary was standing beside me, just watching like the impartial observer he hadn't been. I was about to ask him what was going on and how come he had managed to escape a telling off.

I also wanted to know why anyone needed to be scolded like a child and why Mark had decided that it was up to him to play mother and do all the scolding.

The tussle, between the naughty boy and his Cuban heeled mother, continued outside on the street until I caught up with them both, "Hey hang on, who put you in charge?"

Mark didn't stop to look at me but his voice was direct enough, "I was always in charge."

Friday 16th June 19.00

"So where are we going to next? Is that still up to the two local boys or have you taken charge!"

"Let's go to the Duke of York. It's not far and we're finished here anyway, aren't we, boys"?

"You're starting to sound like the big boy in the playground".

"Is that the big boy who did it and ran away?" taunted Sammy. Mark just shoved him into a lamp post without even breaking step.

"Sorry, Mickey, I didn't mean to spoil the mood. But I was pissed off with Sammy for being so stupid. You can't talk like that when you don't know who is listening. Remember we would never have gone into a pub unless we knew it was a Protestant bar. They had their bars, we had our bars. They stayed out of our bars and we stayed out of theirs.

I would have liked another beer in the John Hewitt, but 'the night was but a pup' as we used to say at the start of a decent session, and no doubt there were more beers and more pubs ahead. I did start to wonder though, if anyone had given any thought to eating at all. I'd had nothing but coffee and scones since landing and was starting to regret the traumatic end suffered by the Paris buns. I was hungry for something to line the stomach at least.

People were starting to gather in the various venues of this new cosmopolitan Belfast. There were narrow roads like pretty Andalucian lanes adorned with hanging flower baskets and benches where the smokers could sit, chat, enjoy their pint and have somewhere to stub out their cigarettes. In my day if you saw someone standing outside a pub, you assumed that they had been thrown out.

I remember Sammy sitting for hours one night on the huge concrete flowerpots outside Montgomery's as he waited for us to finish our beers and accompany him up to the Grouse. Instead we went out through the other entrance and headed in the opposite direction to the George. It was a collective decision as we'd all had enough of his sash bashing rants when he encountered anyone who failed to agree with his demands to repatriate all Catholics to the South of Ireland where he believed they came from originally, even the ones he had known since his Mum put him into St Patricks parish playgroup. The landlord of Montgomery's hadn't shared Sammy's views on Catholics, especially since he had married one, and so Sammy was asked to wait outside. He did. We didn't.

I never really thought about it, but if I had been in Sammy's shoes, I would have given up and looked for other friends. It wasn't as if there weren't plenty of people in Ballymena who shared his views on ethnic diversity. But nobody knew much about ethnic diversity in those days and certainly not people like Sammy. Worse still, we didn't know anybody who did like Sammy, he never seemed to have any other friends. But he was adamant that he was our friend and most definitely Mark's friend.

Sammy and Mark were ahead and leading the way to the next bar, from behind they almost looked as if they were holding hands. Meanwhile Gary was tracking me, as we weaved through the sauntering hordes of pretty young and not so young things beginning to fill the bars for the evening. Mark and Sammy looked the part in their shabby chic of linen and denim which seemed to fit in well with the overall fashion vibe, I looked at Gary and half expected to be disappointed to see him in the old, faded denim jacket that he always wore as a youth. But neither he nor I looked out of place. A jacket, jeans and a loud shirt seemed to go a long way these days.

"Hey what's up with those two? One minute they are ready to explode and the next they are almost hugging each other."

"Mickey surely you remember it was always that way. Sammy looked on Mark as the big brother he always wanted, and Mark had him wrapped around his little finger. We all looked up to Mark, he was the cool one. The one to get first pick of the girls. The one with the latest gear. Do remember his Crombie coat with the red hankie in the breast pocket? That's the way we were. First there was Mark and then there was us. He would have been the blonde guy if we were in Scoobie Doo's gang."

"And Sammy was Thelma or Shaggy?"

"I think Sammy was Scoobie! We even called him that for a while!"

"Hey, Scoobie wait on us!"

We caught up with the other two just as we arrived at the front door of the Duke of York bar. Mark held open the heavy door, "After you ladies!". We shuffled in and made our way to the nearest set of bar mounted taps.

"Yes, gentlemen, what can I do for you?" said a barman with a beard so big and bushy that you would have expected him to be able to wrestle bears and start fires in the woods with just his fingertips and some twigs.

I decided to stake some authority, "Let's make it simpler this time. Four pints of Harp and do you have any crisps? Tayto Crisps?"

"Ah a man of taste and discernment! Have you been away long sir?" grinned the barman, exposing teeth which were much too white for such a hillbilly beard.

"What makes you think I've been away?" I asked as he started to pull the pints.

"Well first it's the accent. Just a little too posh for pure Norn Iron and then it's the old packet of Tayto and pint of Harp combo. You'll be asking if we do an Ulster Fry next!"

I took it in the humour that he intended but I couldn't help but seem a little miffed that even a Belfast barman had recognised me for the obvious tourist that I was. I turned with the first of the two pints and saw that the other three had found a place to sit already. They were already deep in conversation. "I guess I'll get these ones in, then" and I returned to pick up the other two pints and the four yellow bags of the most beautiful potato crisps ever held captive in shiny plastic. I was going to enjoy this.

"D'ya know what that barman said to me just now? He said my accent was too posh to be pure Northern Irish."

"Well, you know what they say about the bar staff in here?" said Mark.

"What?" said both Gary and Sammy at the same time.

"You're not going to like it Sammy, but Gerry Adams used to be a barman in here and he learned all he knows about politics from the banter he overheard in this bar"

"Well he would have learnt it a bit differently if he had been listening to Sammy just now," said Gary.

"Is that right enough?"

"Tis, so it is." Mark and I laughed together.

Friday 16th June 20.00

I liked the Duke of York; it had a lot of character. By that I mean it had a lot of old odd stuff on the walls and ceilings, pictures, metal signs and things that were meant to make you feel nostalgic I suppose. It gave you something to look at when the conversation in your company got a bit boring. But it was cosy too. Nooks and crannies, turns and twists, places to hide if you needed to hide.

I had visited it a few times when I was a student, but usually only in the company of my student friends rather than my hometown friends. In those days, it wasn't the sort of place a group of young lads from Ballymena would have felt comfortable. Maybe welcome but not comfortable. Its connections with Sinn Fein leader Gerry Adams and some city centre bomb blasts, had ensured its place in Belfast folklore forever. It seemed inevitable that Sammy would be drawn back to his favourite topic of conversation.

"I hear Snow Patrol, used to come in here a lot, when they were recording their early albums" said Mark clearly hoping for a new thread of conversation.

"Never liked them!" snapped a grouchy Sammy.

"I like their stuff and so does the missus. We went to see them live a few years back," said Gary.

"I think I have a few of their albums?" I said, "Where did you see them play, Gary?"

"To hell with Snow Patrol. What did you just say about Gerry Adams working in here?" interrupted Sammy.

"Don't worry Sammy, he's got a better job these days and has been too busy to do a full shift for a while now." replied Mark immediately, still trying to move things on.

"To think that murdering scumbag could have served me a beer."

"Not unless you started drinking very young, Sammy" sneered Mark raising his pint glass to his lips. "Would you wind your neck in, for fuck sake. I'm no fan of the man either but I got over it. It was before our time.

He never did anything on me, that I know of and I'm kinda fed up hearing about how everybody 'did you wrong'. No matter how long ago it was. King Billy's horse once shit in my Granny's garden, but she got over it. Let it lie, man, let it lie."

The huff that followed, allowed us enough time to finish our pint in mutual silence while watching the other patrons of the bar demonstrate what it's like to go out for a night and enjoy themselves. The style in the city had certainly improved since my student days, the women didn't all look as if they were auditioning to have their picture on the back of a can of Tennants lager, and hard man chic of half-mast trousers and inappropriately named bomber jackets had been left in the closet of the past.

"Another pint then?" offered Gary standing to his feet and squeezing out to make his way to the bar.

"Aye, but when were we thinking of getting something to eat." I asked, as I tied the last of the empty crisp bags into a knot and tossed it into the middle of the table.

"I always found it very annoying, the way you used to do that and leave the knotted bag in the ashtray." said Mark but with a wry smile. "You never smoked like the rest of us and you just never got it. How annoying it was to have the ashtray littered up with little knots and bows of crinkly crisp packets. Back in the day, when we could smoke in a pub rather than in the outside smoking area, sitting on a silly wee bench with a gas heater burning the back of your neck and forced to talk to strangers who you had nothing more in common with than a craving for nicotine and maybe a talent for blowing smoke rings."

"Who's getting a bit techy now, big man?" said Sammy, winking at me as he spoke.

"Ah no, it's just a pet hate of mine. In Spain when you eat or drink outside in the restaurants and bars, there are ashtrays in many of the older places and you can still get away with the odd fag."

"Do you still smoke? Aren't you worried about your health?" I asked.

"Smoking is a necessary occupational risk for me!" shrugged Mark.

I had known that there was a long running rumour that Mark had been doing some regular drug deals. I'd seen him smoke dope often enough. In fact, I had even joined him in a few wee tokes occasionally, but I had turned a blind eye when I heard other people talk and when some even described him as a dealer. I doubted if it was ever in large quantities but that was back then and more recently the rumours had even reached me in Edinburgh when I heard that his move to Spain was in some way linked to or even financed by some more substantial exchanges of euro for Mary Jo.

"Yeah, something to eat would be a good idea." said Gary arriving with the first two new pints, he returned with the second two and the additional news that the barman had suggested we try the Dirty Onion, as it had decent food and was just around the corner.

"The Dirty Onion? Is that a bar or a …." sparked up Sammy again.

"Too slow! If you're going to be sarcastically witty, you need to be quicker with your repartee" interrupted Mark.

"That's our Sammy, a master of wit and repartee but only if you've booked in advance." Gary distributed the new pints, and we drank them down like men who had been deprived of refreshment for all of 30 minutes.

The session was gathering momentum and a discussion of food options was now on the agenda. I was flexible but wanted something reasonably healthy although I realised it was going to be difficult to find fast food that wasn't fried. Sammy said he wanted a fish supper, which as I remembered was Norn Irish for fish and chips. Mark didn't seem to care, and Gary suggested a pizza. Seizing on that as the non-fried option, I agreed to go with the pizza. We could get two of them to share between the four of us, if we could ever agree on the toppings.

"No onions or Mushrooms on mine." "Chicken or salami?" "As long as it doesn't have pineapple?" "What fucking kind of pizza has pineapple on it", "One with the word Hawaiian in its name usually, you philistine", "I want a pizza not a fruit salad", "Get yer man, with the special dietary requirements, I'd be happy with a soda filled with brown sauce and some vegetable roll"

We finally agreed on two Margaritas and no extra toppings. Pints were downed in one gulp and we headed for the Dirty Onion.

It wasn't far to walk to the Dirty Onion and there was plenty to look at, as Belfast's brightest who were more fashion than health conscious enjoyed their cigarettes in the narrow street. The bar claims to be Belfast's oldest building and takes shabby chic to extremes, as my mother would have said it could have done with a lick of paint. There were seats, in distressed leather and flaking paint, but most people seemed to be standing around looking to see if anyone else was looking at them. The writing above the entrance to the beer garden claimed the building dated back to 1680, which was just 10 years before the first tattoo was done in Belfast. I could see the other three looking around at the décor and the clientele, and it was obvious that neither made any of us feel at home. We all went to the bar this time, preferring to stay together like the group of outsiders that we obviously were.

"Do you do Harp?" asked Marc.

The barman was overly pleasant for someone whose job was simply to pour pints and take money. The hospitality industry having finally woken up to the old Belfast charm of the last century, might just have overdone it a bit with their 'Welcome' training. He nodded and said he could do us Tenants if we liked but, "To be honest we don't sell a lot of it in here."

"I bet you don't. What about Guinness then? Four pints of Guinness if you could. Surely you sell Guinness? And do you have a food menu I could look at please?"

"No probs mate, four Stout, but if you want food, you'll need to go upstairs to the Yardbird,"

Sammy was out of his comfort zone, his unease and paranoia among strangers had been pushed to the limit. His patience snapped, "I'm not your mate, and I don't want to go upstairs. You can stuff your 'Stout' up your distressed hole." The barman recoiled, quickly lost his hospitality trained smile and reached below the edge of the bar counter.

Sensing the presence of a panic button rather than the more traditional baseball bat of yester year. Mark put his hand firmly on Sammy's shoulder and turned him in the direction of the door. "Thanks, but I think we should go before we are asked to leave." He said calmly to the barman. We were outside before Gary or I had time to appreciate that we had become the centre of attention for the entire bar and not because we looked too old or distressed.

"Do they do pizza upstairs?" pleaded Gary in a last gasp, as his hunger overruled any feeling of commitment to our group's collective discontent. But only for an instant.

A helpful bystander, out of some misplaced sense of neighbourliness or desire to help the confused old men, advised, "They only do chicken upstairs." But then shut up as soon as she saw Sammy's glare and heard him tell her where she needed to insert the chicken to which she referred and how he hoped it would make her eyes water.

It just wasn't our kind of place, neither mine nor Gary's. Definitely not Sammy's but maybe Mark's. I couldn't be sure if he was more annoyed at Sammy's temper tantrum or at having to leave the bar before even getting served and before he'd had enough time to enjoy inspecting the available pretty young things. We were outside again and making our way along the streets towards an old familiar bar. The impressive building that housed Bittle's Bar was looming up ahead and our need for another beer had taken precedence over the previous search for food. Or more specifically food other than chicken.

The red bricked narrow tower was Belfast's smaller version of New York's Flat Iron building and presented an unusually narrow frontage put a pleasant interior. This was an old man's pub. People came here to talk. Talk about poetry and literature and culture and politics and things that intelligent people talk about. No doubt we would feel more at home in here. No doubt at all.

I knew the bar from my student days, when it looked as grubby as the Dirty Onion was trying to look today, but without the same pretentiousness. It was a great bar for an honest pint in the afternoon. A good place to calm a boy's growing tensions. I pulled Mark with me up to the bar. I wasn't going to bother to ask anyone what they wanted to drink. This time we would get whatever the barman offered and as quickly as he could serve it. Thankfully, Sammy and Gary found a seat for us easily enough. I felt that we needed to take a few minutes just to talk. To take stock of ourselves and chill.

"What is up with Sammy?" I asked Mark, while we waited for the four pints to be poured.

"There's a lot of old bitterness in him and it's not just his old traditional bigotry. I've tried talking to him, but I think his neck is on some kind of spring. No sooner than he's told to wind it in, than something sets him off and he springs back in everyone's face."

"Is it something one of us has done?"

"I'll try and explain it to you when I get the chance. Just humour him for now."

We took our seats at the back of the long room. This was more like it. Four pints of unbranded lager in glasses that didn't need a corporate logo to explain the taste. A round tin ashtray wouldn't have looked out of place even if it had no practical use to the smokers forced to smoke outside. A rolled up copy of the Belfast Telegraph would have helped complete the old memories forming in my head, as well as being useful as a wedge to stabilise the wobbly table. I felt as if I needed to reach into my pockets for my packet of twenty Marlboro Lights and one pound lighter, and place them in a little stack on the small round Formica table to stake my claim.

But I hadn't smoked for years, maybe twenty or more years, since my daughter asked me to stop because she didn't want her daddy to die. I wouldn't even consider myself to be an ex-smoker anymore. I just didn't smoke. Smoking had nothing to do with me. I was more interested in my health. Determined to stay alive. Scared of dying.

Friday 16th June 21.00

"So how are we all keeping? You're all looking pretty good anyway. Have we all been flirting with the Lycra?" I asked, hoping to find a non-contentious topic of conversation.

"I wear Lycra shorts and stuff like that when I'm out cycling, if that's what you mean," said Sammy completely oblivious to my sarcasm.

"So, do you go out riding much then?" Mark said laughing at his own joke, but on his own.

"I go out a few times each week on my own and then I do a big ride at the weekend with some of the guys from work."

"I bet you do!"

"I bought a bike, but never felt comfortable on it. They're bloody dangerous too. Have you ever fallen off one of those things, you'd be lucky to get away with skinning your knees", moaned Gary.

"I've got a mountain bike, that I keep in the cellar in Spain, but I don't bother much with it anymore. Too bloody clammy for cycling up all those hills, especially with a belly full of wine. I do run though, mostly in the gym, on a treadmill," said Mark.

"Yeah, I used to run a lot, I even did a few 10ks but never got as far as a marathon. Mostly I swim now, it's easier on the joints apparently." I said.

"In the sea?"

"Have you ever been in the sea in Scotland? No way, obviously I meant the local pool. Every morning except Sunday. Well almost every morning."

"My god listen to us. The last of the great Olympians. As I remember it, we would have gone to any lengths to get out of PE at school, and I don't recall any of us playing for any of the school teams at anything," said Sammy.

"Mickey and I both played for the chess team ", said Mark.

"The pinnacle of physical prowess, nerds on steroids, I don't remember that." laughed Sammy.

"No, you needed a brain to be allowed to join the chess club. I was more of a cross country running sort of guy. I still do the occasional run but nothing competitive. Just me and her out on a Sunday morning maybe," said Gary.

"That's nice!" sneered Sammy. "I don't cycle for the fun of it, but you need to do something at our age. It keeps me fit and that's it. To hell with the social side and don't ever let my wife know that Gary and his missus run together. I don't need mine out riding with me."

"We know!" Gary chipped in.

"Yip, always the team player, that was you Sammy and never one to go riding with a woman when the boys from work were about," said Mark with a smile.

"Leave it!" I spluttered into my pint. "I guess we are all trying to stay alive then, it's just a pity that we weren't into sports at school. Who knows where it might have led?"

"Yeah, I could have been a contender! Top of the world ma! A champion! An international superstar," taunted Mark.

"You did ok, Mark. We all did. Maybe not as sporting legends, but we're all still alive and no one seems to be heading for the emergency department just yet," said Gary.

"Well maybe but I need to explain something. I have this irregular heartbeat thing. I get palpitations and need treatment sometimes when my heart rate speeds up too much. It's called cardio arrhythmia" I confessed.

"Could it kill you?" said Gary, shocked beyond the application of any hint of subtlety.

"It could, yes, but when they take me into hospital to treat me, they actually stop my heart before restarting it again at the 'correct' rhythm. So, in effect it has already caused me to die, if you count death as being whenever your heart stops. But that's not the way I'm supposed to think about it. It's all under control, I just have to be careful and know when to slow down or go to see a medic."

"Tablets and all?"

"Yip"

"Nice!"

" Let's go for some chips."

Friday 16th June 21.30

Chips might not have been what I should have been having, but I had to admit the guilty pleasure was very enticing. I knew I shouldn't but no one back at home would ever know and these three didn't seem to care much, despite my revelation about my heart condition. One visit to the legendary Long's chip shop, over behind the Europa Hotel, wouldn't hurt? Anyway, it would be worth it. No one ever forgets their first time at Longs and appropriately enough my first time was on the same night that I lost my virginity. I was a first-year student at Queen's University and hadn't realised that some girls could be enticed into bed with only a promise of a fish supper and a few beers. She was a student too. Not from Belfast but living away, from her home in Derry. Most students went home for the weekend, back to get their washing done and to eat some real food, but the hardcore types would stay up over the weekend which was a time to be a bit more adventurous. She was also a first year on the same course as me and we had got to know each other after I had offered her a piece of my chewing gum. "Umm Juicy Fruit" was her answer and enough for me to appreciate her sense of humour. That night it ended up with just the two of us walking around the University area on a bit of a pub crawl, visiting the bars we knew were safe enough for students to visit and cheap enough for us to be able to afford to drink. She suggested Long's chip shop as a proper way to finish the night and who was I to argue. We walked back up to the Student Halls of residence and the fish and chips lasted for the entire journey. Having chatted intensely to each other for most of the evening mostly about movies, the consumption of the last few chips and the large, battered cod, brought a welcome respite from conversation. I thought she just wanted to resume our discussion of how Mickey Rourke was shit at the Northern Irish accent, but when I accepted her offer to come in for a coffee, I didn't expect, that we would be having it along with a post coital cigarette. I didn't even smoke, but thought it would be rude to refuse, given what she had just allowed me to do. Like I say, I've never forgotten my first fish supper from Long's nor the events thereafter.

The walk from Bittle's bar to Long's Chip Shop, took us past the impressive City Hall. But then again doesn't everywhere have an impressive City Hall. It's just that you think your hometown has the best, until you travel elsewhere and get to compare a few others. We often believe that our own wee country is better than everywhere else. The city was now better at lighting up its public spaces. The city centre might never be as vibrant as it should be, but at least it appeared less intimidating than those bad old days when it was somewhere you imagined could end up as a headline on the morning news as journalist W D Flax reported on the discovery of a body of a young person in a shop doorway in Royal Avenue. The four of us walked together this time, as if we were a bit unsure of who or what we might bump into on the way.

"My Fitbit just buzzed. That's my 10,000 steps for the day," announced Gary, looking pleased with himself.

"I don't think it counts if you measure a pub crawl as part of your daily exercise. Anyway, those things are no good" said Sammy.

"I've got one as well," said Mark "and Mickey has a pacemaker. Don't you Mickey?"

"No, I don't, that isn't part of the treatment. I had a Fitbit for a while after my first procedure, but I stopped wearing it because it was depressing." I said.

"Can't take the pace, Big Man. That was always you. No stamina." said Sammy.

"Shut the fuck up Sammy." I replied.

Long's was within sight and I didn't need Sammy to give me another reason to feel more guilty about my impending indulgence in nostalgia and fried carbohydrate.

"Four fish suppers, salt and vinegar on them all, please. It's my round." Mark was first to the counter and no one felt a need to decline his offer. "Anyone want anything to drink with that or will we just wait and get another pint somewhere, when we've finished?"

"Aye, we can sit and watch the great unwashed of Belfast while we eat, and maybe finish with a pint in the Crown bar before heading home."

"Aye, good idea."

It looked like we had a plan at last and maybe there might even be a sensible end to our night on the town in Belfast. We all seemed to welcome that idea.

Sitting on a low wall on Great Victoria Street on a Friday night, with a portion of fish and chips, while watching the rest of the world getting on with their start to the weekend, seemed a million miles away from my memories of Belfast in the 1980's. It just wasn't something you would have done back then, and now it seemed very ordinary, even pedestrian. Just four old friends trying to understand how they had ever got this old and maybe even feeling relived that just being alive was some measure of success.

Friday 16th June 22.30

I probably hadn't noticed him until some sixth sense nudged me to realise that someone was watching me, when eventually it kicked in and I became aware that there was a someone staring at me from across the road. He could have been waiting for a taxi, but there was something about the way he was standing. Very upright. Very still. Very focussed on us, or maybe, more on me. To stare at a stranger late at night on Victoria Street, wasn't a good idea, no matter who you were, but he didn't seem to be bothered that I was now looking back at him and just like that moment when you make accidental eye contact with a stranger, I was now feeling uncomfortable. But he didn't seem to share my anxiety. I avoided his fixed stare and took more effort than necessary to find a particular chip that might be just able to rescue me from the growing awkwardness. But I did look back at him. I had to. He was still there, still staring, still motionless. Like a ghost from the past projected onto an unfamiliar future.

So, what else could I do. I nodded and said, "What about ye, big lad? Alright?"

He nodded back and started crossing the road towards me. I straightened myself up and pushed out my chest. I was ready for him. To be sure, I also flicked my foot against the back of Mark's leg, to draw his attention to the developing situation and the imminent arrival of our new friend. Mark turned around to suggest that I should 'watch where you're poking your big fucking feet', when our new friend came close enough to announce, "I thought it was you".

"Who me? Do I know you?"

"Not you. Him. The big man there."

So, it wasn't me that our young friend had been staring at but Mark.

"Aye you. Don't you remember me?"

Mark was now fully aware that he was the centre of someone's attention and had turned around to directly confront the owner of the inquisitive Belfast accent.

"I don't think so mate. Who the fuck are you anyway? What makes you think you know me?"

Sammy and Gary were now also rising to their feet ready to join in on the potential standoff, like two hired bodyguards preparing to protect their boss from whatever might be about to happen.

"Oh, I know you. And him too," pushing his finger in the direction of Sammy's rapidly reddening face.

"You used to know my Dad. You'd be round our house way back in the day. I was only wee but I remember you two. You'd go out with him on jobs and everything."

Mark seemed suddenly composed but at the same time defensive. "Sorry mate I don't recognise you. Who did you say your Dad was? Where did you say we worked together?"

"I didn't say you worked together and I'm sure you remember my Da. They say, I'm his double, and everyone on this side of Belfast, knew my Da back then. Just the same as everybody knows me now."

I could see Sammy was about to step forward, but Mark's outstretched arm stopped him in his tracks. "I'm sorry son you must have the wrong guys. We're not from around here and anyway that's our taxi now."

A taxi had just pulled up and the driver was in the process of winding down the window of the cab to announce, "Taxi for White", when Mark opened its back doors, pushed Sammy onto the rear seats and shouted at me to "get another cab and we'd all meet up at the Hotel."

Gary looked at me with big wide eyes and hunched shoulders. He was clearly as much in the dark about what was going on as I was. I looked at the young guy still stood in front of us. He was glaring in the direction of the taxi. It was making an abrupt turn into the evening traffic and the three of us stood in silence until they disappeared into the city traffic.

"It was him. I know it was him. Tell your mate when you see him 'back at the hotel' that Billy's son would really like to catch up with him for a chat. I'm glad to know that he's back in Northern Ireland, even if it might be only briefly, but I'd be really keen to see him again. Wherever it suits him"

"Billy? Billy who? Isn't half of this bloody town called Billy?"

"Sorry, but I've just run out of business cards, anyway I'm sure old Marky boy will know who I mean. Just tell him Protestant Billy's little boy Kenny, is all grown up now."

I don't think he was expecting me to respond, which was good, because I couldn't find any words. Not that there wasn't plenty of questions swirling around my head, but not one single word had the slightest chance of making its way to my lips. Gary appeared to have similarly pressed his personal pause button. Our new friend however calmly raised his hand to hail another taxi, gave us one last disparaging look and without a further word left us standing like two sixteen-year-old virgins on a first trip to a lap dancing club.

"What just happened!"

"Dunno!"

"What was that about?"

"Dunno!"

"Should we be worried?"

"I don't fucking know! I'm all done with your questions. Can we get a taxi now? Please?"

"Keep your hair on!"

I stuck my hand in the air drawing the immediate attention of one of the cars waiting on the Europa Hotel's informal taxi rank. A white Mercedes moved forward and the window rolled down.

"Will you drive us to Ballymena mate?"

"Popular place tonight? No problem. Get in."

Friday 16th June 23.00

I've always enjoyed being driven somewhere at night. Whether by a friend or by a taxi driver. But in both situations, it was the quietness I would enjoy. The solitude of silence as you got to watch the night landscape roll past without being responsible for the journey. The freedom to be able to imagine the stories unfolding behind the lights of buildings as they rushed forward and passed as quickly from view. People at home with their loved ones, doing what was normal for them. People living alone and coping with the loneliness by doing whatever they convinced themselves was normal and usually wasn't. To my mind, cities at night look so calm. I never saw them as something exciting nor scary, just calm, full of people getting on with life. Was that naive of me to think like that? Or just optimistic. Just because I like to imagine that people might be trying to do their best and live their lives without deliberately trying to hurt others, doesn't make me delusional. I do know that badness does happen in the world. I grew up in Northern Ireland for goodness sake. But it rarely happens to me or mine. I might have avoided contact with the worst of our 'Troubles' but I wasn't ignorant of what was going on around me.

The quietness in the taxi, that had until now, allowed me to indulge in this kind of personal philosophy, was about to be interrupted. Gary had been engaging in his own quiet reflection as well, but I hadn't really noticed until now. It was the taxi driver who cracked the silence. "Where are we going to, once we reach Ballymena. North or South?"

"Neither. Take us to the Adair Arms Hotel. That's about as central as you can get in Ballymena." said Gary. "So don't take the by-pass at the next roundabout."

We were closer to the town than I had realised. Maybe another ten minutes would have us there. It was barely midnight.

"Are we supposed to be meeting those two at the Hotel for a nightcap or something?" I asked.

"I doubt it Mickey. I would have liked another wee drink myself, but I suspect that Sammy will be well on his way home and I got the impression that Mark wasn't in the mood for a chat either."

"Yeah, what was that all about? Who was the young Guy? Do you think Mark or Sammy knew him?"

"Listen Mickey, I don't know what it was about, but I do know that Mark did have a bit of a history that he prefers to keep to himself. We both have our doubts about how he made his money, but he must have started somewhere. You and I had other things on our mind at the end of the seventies and I just never asked. If he wants to tell you, he will. But you can be sure that Sammy wasn't a saint back then either and he certainly won't be saying anything without Mark's approval."

"What sort of stuff are you talking about?"

"Like I said, you need to ask him yourself, if you must, but then again why bother. The past is the past. It's a different place. Isn't it?"

The taxi pulled up at the front door of the hotel and even though it was still early for a Friday night, there didn't seem to be much life about the place. Certainly nothing compared to the days of Bentley's disco, when the front bar would have been full of our kind of people 'getting a few in' before heading into the disco in the function room at the rear of the hotel. There was no sign of Mark or Sammy either.

As we entered the hotel foyer, Gary was putting away his phone. "That's her on her way. She'll be here in two minutes. Not much point in waiting around is there?"

"Obviously bloody not! What's wrong with you guys? I was looking forward to having a few late nights during this stag weekend. Isn't that one of the benefits of staying in a hotel that you can take full advantage of the night bar?"

"Mickey let's just call it a night for tonight. We still have tomorrow."

"We've got tonight babe, who needs tomorrow. Who are you, Bob Seger?"

"I'm just not used to lots of drinking anymore. It's been a good night though and hopefully those other two will be feeling a bit fresher and friendlier tomorrow. What time do you want to meet up, anyway?"

"I think we said twelve. Ok goodnight. Maybe you're right, a good night's sleep wouldn't do any harm."

I turned to make my way towards the staircase and eventually my room. I saw Gary hold his phone to his ear again as he walked out the front door of the hotel and onto the street beyond. I could see the headlights of a car as it pulled up beside him. Obviously, his wife had arrived to take him home.

I didn't even bother to check if Mark had already got in. He certainly wasn't in the bar. No one was.

Tomorrow was another day. We got things to do, we got eggs to lay. We got ground to dig and worms to scratch …. and there was nobody here but us.

Saturday 17th June 01.00

I got into bed and was tempted to keep my socks on. It wouldn't have looked very sexy but who would ever know. I fell asleep quite quickly, serenading myself with Louis Jordan's back catalogue.

My dreams are usually tuned into in the seventies, which must say something about the life I've led and the regrets I've accumulated or else that's just the channel I prefer to watch. This time I was still whistling, 'there ain't nobody here but us chickens' as they led me into the dock. I was instructed to stand in the dock on my own. It reminded me of a church pew, as they closed what looked like a wooden gate at the end of my own little wooden corridor. I expected to see a velvet padded bench for me to sit on, but instead it was a simple wooden stool. It didn't look very stable and I doubted if it could bear my weight for long. So, I chose to stand. I took a look around the courthouse. It wasn't very big, maybe the size of a tennis court, but cluttered with many levels of dark wood, benches, tables and other pews, most of which were empty. The walls didn't look as if they had a colour, but I guess that's why Magnolia is so popular. In the corner above the door that I had just come through, where the walls met the ceiling, there were signs of flaking paint, as if the corner was damp or the source of a leak. Come to think of it, there was a smell of dampness, or maybe I was just expecting that to be the case.

Across the court room from where I was standing and therefore directly in my gaze, was another wooden pew. But it was longer than mine and big enough to accommodate the two rows 12 people, all dressed in some kind of ermine edged red robes. It looked as if they were missing their tricorn hats, to complete the olde town crier look. The smell of moth balls from the robes added to the overall unpleasant odour. They all stood up simultaneously like well-behaved children, as their master, the Judge entered from another door, which I hadn't noticed before. I became aware of a kerfuffle behind me as my friends and relatives in yet another set of crowded pews, adjusted themselves as they thought was appropriate and necessary.

We were such a bid-able family, always eager to be seen to do the right thing, though never sure of who decided what was right.

Then I noticed the shadowy figure addressing the Judge. He described himself as the lawyer for the prosecution and announced to the attentive courtroom that he was going to consider my past and how I might have developed as a child destined to under achieve and misbehave.

He retold stories of how as a young man, I was always reluctant to attend Sunday School and those regular wee mid-week meetings where men with too much nasal hair and dressed in stale smelling grey suits, would terrify me with their unfounded descriptions of Judgement day and my inevitable journey to hell. If it was as inevitable as they all predicted, why did we even bother with all those meetings? I just didn't have the makings of a good Christian. I suppose I just asked too many questions. This curious child was surely hell-bound. The shadowy lawyer went on to tell how my mysterious childhood illness had been sent as retribution for my doubting curiosity. That loving God certainly knew how to teach a child a lesson. The sins of my youth would haunt me forever and I would always be in debt to the church, I was soulless and needed to make financial recompense. Prayer alone wouldn't be enough to correct my failings of the past. I heard someone from the other public benches behind me, mutter "Aye, he was always difficult, too clever for his own good but not as good as the other boys in his class.", "Aye, if only he had been like the rest of us?"

The lawyer continued with his testimony. I had been spoilt as a child, a favourite who was always given more opportunity than he perhaps deserved. Gifted maybe but could have done better, if he hadn't wasted all those opportunities, he could have been a doctor maybe or a politician. Someone who could have made a difference in the world. He reminded the courtroom of my involvement in a successful school team in an economics challenge to run a successful business in a computer simulated game against other schools across N. Ireland. The other members of the team had been much cleverer than I was, but I was able to benefit from the reflected glory of their abilities, which was allegedly what I'd done throughout my adult life. I prefer to believe that even though the superior intelligence of my fellow team-mates was beyond question, I was valued for a different type of non-academic intelligence. I was good at something even if others didn't think so.

I looked across at my accuser, but he had been replaced by another figure, a larger man, taller and more of a presence in the room. But I still couldn't make out his facial features. He lifted his hooded head from the papers in front of him and began to address the attentive congregations in the pews. They strained forward, eager to receive their next intake of gossip. What could they expect to hear now? What salacious opinions were they about to get to chew on. No doubt, whatever it was, they would enjoy the opportunity to make comparisons with their own circumstances and their own feelings of righteousness.

"He's not well, in fact unlike the rest of us, he is getting himself ready to die. He stands alone, as his life reaches its conclusion. Soon he will be judged before our god and asked to explain why he never achieved the requisite 2.4 children and semi-detached mortgage. Is he not content with his annual two weeks of happiness in the Mediterranean? Who does he think he is, to want more than everyone else. The rest of us are content to get a little something for ourselves but he wanted it all. Could he not be content with his lot and just wait to die like the rest of us? Ready for eternity. As we sit here in this courtroom, why should he be allowed to expect more from life, than us? I don't think he was one of us at all.", said the imposing accuser in the midst of the courtroom.

The public gallery behind me, shuffled in unison and collectively sighed as if satisfied that their tribal rituals had been sufficiently acknowledged and once again they all knew that they were right and didn't need any further confirmation of their beliefs.

The accuser seemed to have satisfied himself that he had said all he needed to say. The collective complicity of the pews gave him all the confidence he needed. He was seamlessly replaced by a third figure, now taking his position as the lawyer for the prosecution before the bench. He commenced by informing the judge that his job was to consider the future. Or more accurately my future. He seemed pretty confident that my future was already well established. Pre-destined even. He started to explain that my eventual demise was an acceptable 'Joyful Suffering', the sort of thing any Presbyterian could reasonably expect as they neared the end.

I had had enough and finally found enough strength to speak up for myself and declare my objection to these presumptive accusations. "Surely, I still have a choice. I can still control my own destiny. I don't have to just fade away and die quietly. I can still make every day count and live a life full of love and happiness."

I had started an argument with the judge, maybe not the norm in a courtroom but acceptable in a dream. Everyone had gone, dissipated as easily as each of the three prosecution lawyers had arrived. There was no one left listening to my pleas, no one cared enough to listen. There was no one left, who needed to be convinced. I faced the judge, alone. Comfortably alone. Just him and I in an empty room which now looked more like the inside of a barn. "So, why should I believe anything you say? Who gave you the right to make the rules?"

I could see the Judge's face quite clearly. He reminded me of someone I knew from my past, but I just couldn't decide who.

I was struggling to put a name to the face and also struggling to breathe. I tossed and turned before waking up feeling breathless and lightheaded. Past experience of many restless nights had taught me that it was best to get up and take a few appropriate tablets washed down with a glass of cold tap water. Even though I hate walking over hotel bedroom carpets in my bare feet.

It was always very satisfying to get back into bed, pull up the duvet and resume my sleep. No matter how hard you tried, it was always impossible to resume your dream, where you had left off. I would never discover the identity of my Judge.

Instead, I dreamt that I was in a parked car in Ahoghill. It was late. Dark but not too dark, wet but not raining. It wasn't my car but judging by the seat I was sitting in; I was doing the driving.

Gary and Sammy had got out of the car, saying that they needed to go for a pee, leaving just Mark and I in the car. We didn't speak. We didn't need to. We just enjoyed the scent from the little green tree dangling from the rear-view mirror above the dashboard. It's a smell, I still detest to this day. As always, silence makes time move more slowly and it seemed a long time had passed since the other two had left the car and disappeared around the corner. Too long to be explained away, as time for "a quick piss". I thought I heard a sound, like repeated muffled thuds. I think Mark had heard it too, judging by the way he straightened himself up in the seat. Almost immediately I saw the other two come running back around the corner, apart from being in a hurry, they seemed to be breathing overly heavily as they got into the back seat of the car and pulled the doors hurriedly shut. Gary said something about needing a pee. That didn't make sense. Whereas Sammy just slapped the back of my seat and said, "Ok, that's it. Let's get moving." I happily obliged and then we were on our way. I didn't appreciate the way he had slapped the back of my seat, as if he was instructing a donkey to get a move on. And I even doubted if he had taken time to either wash or wipe his hands. I started driving in the direction of Portglenone but then doubled back so that I could drop everyone back home into town. It didn't seem to have been an unusual end to a night out with my mates but it didn't seem quite right either.

I'd had this dream many times before and it never felt right. It could vary sometimes. Sometimes the car was still running, sometimes I felt very cold. Sometimes the green tree wasn't the worst smell in the car. But it was a dream that kept coming back and never came to any conclusion. It never ended up with everyone, including me, at home.

I did however remember hearing a siren and soon realised that it was the alarm on my phone. The entire dream melted away and I was back in my hotel room, worrying about setting my bare feet back on the hotel carpet again.

Saturday 17th June 08.00

I don't usually remember any particular dreams but on wakening up to my phone's alarm at 8:00 a.m., I immediately began a post-mortem of the events of the night before. I lay in bed for a good ten minutes, staring at some very disturbing footprints on the bedroom ceiling while re-running the various parts of last night that I could remember or even wanted to remember. I suppose I really wanted to remember it all. This whole trip back to Ballymena and meeting up with the lads, was all about remembering the past or at least giving my memories a bit of a reboot. I had been away for too long and as my mother would say, it was never advisable to forget the 'bowl you were baked in'.

There did appear to be parts of my memories that were missing or at least didn't match up with how the other three remembered everything. I had lived in Ballymena for a little over a year after graduating from Queens University, before heading over to Glasgow to study Dentistry. For my three years as a student in Belfast, I had stayed in student accommodation during the week and returned most weekends although not every weekend. Sammy and Gary had got jobs relatively quickly in the town and enjoyed being single and cash rich. Mark had hung around Belfast and did a variety of part time jobs that must have paid him well enough, as he was the first one of us to have his own car. Maybe it was because I had removed myself from them, that had created the gaps in my memories of our times together. I certainly don't remember any specific time when we all stopped hanging out together, or even a reason why, but I certainly must have been the first to leave, since the three of them had more memories in common than I had.

I needed to get up. I was over thinking it all and those footprints on the ceiling were starting to bother me. What would people be doing in a hotel room that resulted in footprints on the ceiling? I've done strange things in hotel bedrooms in my younger days, but even I wasn't that good or that adventurous.

A quick shower followed by a shave was as much of a pre breakfast routine as I felt the day needed. I would normally do some sit ups and a two-minute plank each morning at home but planking in a hotel bedroom seemed too much of a cliché, to be contemplated by a middle-aged man on his own. The choice of a pair of jeans and a white t-shirt was an appropriate nod to the retro couture of my youth and adequate for breakfast in a room full of strangers. There are few places where you can be more sure of being judged than in the breakfast room of a modern day hotel. People with their mouths full of enough readily available carbohydrates to sustain them until the middle of next week, have little else to do than to measure up their dining companions against their own personal standards. Any measurement, from how high you pile you plate or how often you return to breakfast buffet, to the likelihood of your clothes being the same ones you were wearing last night when you left the bar. I enjoy people watching as much as anyone else but sometimes you know that when sitting at a table for one, you become a target for special attention as the odd one out. The lonely soul who can't be easily put into one pigeon-hole or another. In our wee country, we like to know as soon as possible if you're one of us or one of them.

I was looking forward to my fry. My Ulster Fry. Even better it wasn't coming from the buffet, it would be served to my table. Or so said the pretty waitress who arrived at my table with the tea and coffee pots. She smiled and offered me a choice of continental from the buffet or the full fry. At least she didn't use that awful phrase, "The Full English".

The plate duly arrived, with all the necessary ingredients. Eggs, bacon, sausage, potato bread, soda bread and beans. No. Ah for fuck sake. Beans! They were even touching the potato bread and oozing dangerously close to the fried egg. "That's disgusting! I couldn't eat that, love. You may as well take it back. I'll just have the coffee and toast."

The waitress looked at me, as if I had just spoken to her in a foreign language. "I no understand sir. Why you unhappy with your breakfast. It is not what you ordered?"

"It's not your fault love. It's years of tradition, mixed with an expectation of the familiar and spoiled by the addition of an unnecessary foreign body. What's new?"

She walked away shaking her head. Bloody English beans spoil everything, was what we were both thinking.

There must be somewhere in the town that still served a proper fry. I didn't know if the Daisy Mae café was still open, but I was going to make my way in that direction to find out.

Back in the room, I collected a jacket and took two of my tablets. I'd had the presence of mind to charge my phone and knew it would be a good time to make the obligatory call back to the homestead. It was a phone call that served many purposes but didn't need much time to accomplish any of them. I needed to check that no disaster had befallen my heirs and assets and she needed to know that I was still breathing and to remind me to take enough medication to remain sufficiently alive and able to continue earning a good income. Less than a minute confirmed everything was in order and the call ended with one or other of us saying "I do too". Neither of us had heard any suspicious noises in the background during the call, so that satisfied another unspoken but important function of the call. It wasn't that we didn't trust each other but the last thing you wanted to hear in the background of a call like that, was an unfamiliar voice saying "Hurry up and come back to bed, Darling."

Saturday 17th June 09.30

It was almost 9:30 a.m. in the morning. A dry and sunny Saturday in the market town which was already busy with shoppers and curious onlookers, all wondering what was new. As a child, a trip "up the town" was a regular feature of a Saturday, more a social occasion than the need to perform any hunter gatherer duties. More time would be spent talking to a variety of family acquaintances than spending hard earned and scarce cash. Years later as a young adult, "going into town", filled a similar social function except that you went with your mates rather than your mum or your granny.

"Going into town" was as much an answer to a question from your mates, as it was as a plan of action. As a town, Ballymena was no different to many others in N. Ireland in the late seventies, in that it had little to offer a young man waiting to turn twenty years old. On any Saturday night you had a choice between a few evangelical youth clubs or an occasional under rigorous public house. Both were equally zealous about converting you to their respective versions of salvation. As I remember it, I graduated from the former to the latter, exchanging the threat of violence from the tolerated sectarian bullies of my own 'sort', or church elders as they preferred to be called, for the more managed intimidation of the various paramilitary red necks who were employed as doormen at some of the more popular bars. For some reason 'our crowd' had always managed to avoid any conflict with the various doormen who held the key to a successful Saturday night in County Antrim. No matter which bar we choose to visit, at least one of the four of us would be on speaking terms with one of the bouncers. Mark seemed to have the best networks among the town centre bars, while Sammy was more useful around the events that were run in halls and clubs in the countryside. We might start the evening in a bar in the centre of town with nothing more than a decent jukebox before moving on to arrive fashionably late at a BBQ in some Orange Hall or a disco at the local gun club. Although Sammy's dress sense meant that he had never arrived anywhere fashionably late.

For the rest of us fashion was determined by a limited budget and the buying policy of Sam's Boutique, supplier of teen fashion to the local sheep herd. A trip into town on a Saturday always included a visit to Sam's to browse the branded denim jeans, skinny fit college jumpers, printed shirts with matching ties, zipped jackets with red tartan lining and brogues in every colour of black.

I found myself walking towards the town centre where I expected to see Sam's Boutique at the bottom of Wellington Street. It was still there. A bit posher and a lot more stylish than I remember it, but it was good to know that it was still open and hadn't suffered the same fate as most of the other shops in that lower end of town. Wellington Street was a busy shopping street renowned for its width, where, to my knowledge no sausage had ever actually been tossed in an attempt to make a lewd comparison with an ex-girlfriend's virtue. The town's main shopping strip comprised a triangle of three streets, that allowed us to do continuous loops until we became either bored or hungry. I found myself following that traditional route, like the homeboy I still was. We would have usually ended up having a burger in Desperate Dan's Café on Ballymoney Street, so that's where I was heading. I didn't feel bored or hungry, but I could always stop for a latte and a toasted panini.

"One milky coffee and a toasted bap, for the gentleman with the acquired Scottish accent and a misplaced sense of himself. "

"Glad to see the place hasn't changed much, Dennis".

I took a seat where I could watch the shoppers and the stuttering traffic, through the steamy windows. It felt very familiar and I felt very comfortable as I waited for the waitress to deliver my order. The coffee was good, the bap was covered in too much butter and riddled with guilt.

Cultural icons like Desperate Dan's sandwich bar exist in every town and in everybody's memory. Maybe they weren't the scene of any notable or significant events, although this was where Sammy first spoke to a catholic girl while waiting for a tuna, onion and mayo sandwich (he claims he didn't know she was one of 'them'uns' but she was in her school uniform at the time). It wasn't particularly cool nor trendy, although the guy who owned it was a bit older than us yet lived life as if he wasn't. It wasn't as if the food was spectacular. Although the burgers were tasty and cheap, while the tuna, onion and mayo sandwiches were filled to bursting and made for great packing before a night on the beer. But it was safe, a place where you could sit and listen to the Saturday football results come in without worrying who else might be staring at you. Which was strange since the café was just about on the limits of where we would stroll on a Saturday. It was actually a few metres beyond our triangular traditional territory and to go any further along that street would have felt like trespassing onto 'their' territory. In a different era it would have been a great place for spies to meet to exchange secrets.

In Ballymena you chose your friends not because you liked the same things but because you had formed an alliance with someone who disliked the same things, a bit like how the DUP do politics. I had once thought about becoming a pescatarian, but I didn't like the idea of having to attend church twice every Sunday, so I just ended up being Bank of Ireland. Now I'm just an atheist, thank god.

I had enjoyed my time alone with my teenage memories, but time was moving on and I needed to get back to the hotel to meet up with the others. As I moved up to the counter to pay the bill for my not so continental breakfast, I saw someone staring at me from a car stopped in traffic just outside. It was a silver Mercedes just like Sammy's and Mark was sitting in the passenger seat, looking every bit as surprised to see me as I was to see him.

Saturday 17th June 11.30

I knew he'd seen me, but I hesitated for a second before pulling open the heavy glass door and stepping out onto the street. By then their car had managed to find a space further along the street and had pulled into park on the side of the busy street. It looked as if it had pulled in rather than been parked. It looked as if it had been an unplanned manoeuvre, without appropriate use of either rear view mirror or indicators. It looked as if they hadn't really expected see me.

"Finally! We've been looking for you. I thought we agreed to meet up at the hotel this morning".

"No. We agreed to meet at the hotel at lunchtime. It's now only 11:30. I was just about to head back."

"So, what have you been doing? Where have you been? Why didn't you just stay at the hotel?"

"Because Mark, I'm a big boy and I know my way around this town well enough to take a wee look around the place. We used to do this often enough together, maybe you should have come with me this morning, but I didn't see you at breakfast."

"Come on, we'll give you a lift back to the hotel." He said with no intention of replying to my belated invite.

"Would you like to pull a sack over my head and push me into the back seat just for old time sake."

"Shut up smart arse and get in. Gary will be waiting for us"

"I doubt it. He was never early for anything."

I got into the car. I would have preferred to have walked back on my own, but I didn't see any point in arguing with them. They seemed to be very sure of their intentions. If they had been looking for me, it was mission accomplished but if they had bumped into me by chance, then I was an unanticipated and unwelcome interruption. Whatever they had been doing was now done. Was I becoming a nuisance?

"Don't let me disturb you guys. I'd hate to spoil the party, seeing as how I didn't get an invite to this morning's tour."

"Don't be daft, we were out looking for you. That's all. Sammy came over early. I met him in the hotel reception and when we asked for you, the receptionist said she had seen you go out on your own."

"Where did you go?" asked Sammy.

"Down memory lane, I suppose. I was kind of looking for a decent breakfast and found myself reminiscing about our old Saturdays. Walking around the town, waiting and hoping for something interesting to happen and remembering old school days."

Ballymena has a number of good schools both Secondary and Grammar. But like so many other things in Northern Ireland, there are schools for them'uns and separate ones for us'uns. Any cross fertilization is frowned upon unless it involves a clash of different sports bags at ten spaces in the town bus station. Religious Education is a popular subject in all schools, or so the teachers and parents believe. In reality, pupils rarely know anything of other world religions and prefer instead to debate the various ways to blame the other side for the 'Troubles'. A subject which was always considered best suited to Religious Education rather than History class.

"Good times" replied Sammy.

"Sometimes." added Mark.

"What do you mean?" I tried to look into Mark's eyes, but his tinted glasses made it difficult. As usual.

"I mean that it wasn't always fun back in those days. Sure, we had plenty of laughs, but sometimes it was tough. Sometimes it was dangerous," said Mark.

"Sometimes it was scary," moaned Sammy.

"You could tell me about it if you wanted, but you two are so bloody secretive. You always were in fact. Maybe I do see our past through rose tinted glasses, maybe I didn't experience those days to the same extent as you did, but unless someone writes a book about it, I'll never know all your strange little stories from 'back in the days'"

"Aye and which one of us is ever going to write a book?"

"You never know."

Saturday 12th June 12.00

Sammy pulled the Merc up right outside the front door of the Hotel. Parking spaces that good, only ever happen in the movies, except on this occasion, Sammy had the benefit of ignorance on his side plus the insufficiency of the road markings budget. We had almost parked on a double yellow line but the paintwork would never have stood up in a court.

Gary was on the front steps of the hotel before any of the three of us had managed to groan our way out of the Merc's plush leather seats.

"Don't bother your tired old bones, guys. Let's go. I'm ready" smiled Gary as he pulled open the door of the car.

"Thanks Gary, but I can manage and anyway I need to pick up a different jacket from my room. Give me a few minutes. Anyway, it will give Mark and Sammy sometime to get their story straight. I think I 'shopped their meeting' earlier."

"Sorry, I don't get you" said Gary standing back to let me get out of the car.

I hurried up the steps, shouting back at a puzzled Gary. "You can ask them yourself, what they're up to. They won't tell me"

I was back within less than five minutes, to find the three of them sitting in silence and looking like chastised children, under threat of no tea if they made any more noise. Even Mark was unusually quiet, greeting me with no more than a forced smile, as I got into the passenger seat beside him. He started the car straight away.

"So why are you driving?" I asked as I wondered out loud why Sammy appeared to have lost authority over his own vehicle.

"Cos, I know where we are going."

We drove into the traffic with more conviction than the other road users would have appreciated. Those two really need to pay a bit more attention to their use of car indicators.

We drove along Linenhall Street. It wasn't as busy as it used to be. The poor state of the shop frontages made it all the more obvious that this part of town had suffered from the recent economic collapse and the enforced changes in traffic flow. At least the new town hall, gave the good town's people something to be proud of, although I suspect they might have appreciated a few more play parks for their kids rather than one big glass and concrete play zone for the towns better connected elite.

There are no politics in Ballymena, as the town's people seem to have re-elected the same person ever since the sixties. It's similar to North Korea's aristocracy where successive family members appear to get continually re-elected despite rarely being seen in public. Apparently, it's an idea that emerged in Asia, somewhere near the Maldives. Historically politicians have issues with authority, their own mostly, tending to be a mongrel lifeform of lawyers and preachers.

Mark swung the Merc around the roundabout that would have taken us onto the dual carriageway out of town, and instead drove towards Harryville and eventually the road to Antrim.

Harryville was Ballymena's heartland. Its Protestant Heartland. Anything that was of any importance in Ballymena, had happened in Harryville, or at least started off in Harryville. From protests and arrests, political strikes and marches, even parades and processions, it all happened in Harryville. As I remember, it was where my Dad went to buy his Sunday paper. Which I never understood, because he had to drive past two other newsagents to get there. But that was Harryville. Things happened in Harryville, again and again, just the same way that they always did. Harryville didn't tolerate change in any form. There were a couple of well known, or maybe even notorious bars in that part of town and a well-used bookmakers. I never used either, but I know Mark would have gone into The Raglan Bar in its heyday.

The only place I ever went to on a regular basis was the barber's shop. McCartney's. Where I could be left as a child on a Saturday under the control of Mr William McCartney and his ever present cigarette, while my Dad could flit between the bookies or the bars until I would be released back onto Henry Street and sent to retrieve my Dad. It wasn't as if my Dad was neglecting me or leaving me unattended in any way. Mr McCartney made sure you stayed under control in the barber's chair by continuing to hold his burning cigarette less than two inches from your face while he buzzed and clipped your 'short back and sides'. The stink of the Bay Rum liberally applied to your new hair style, would always mean that you were easily traceable by anyone needing to find you. Other than that, Harryville was just a place that I drove through on my way to somewhere else. And sometimes where I bought my Sunday paper.

Mark was driving as if it was still the seventies and we were on our way to Belfast. The car was a much better one than any we drove back in the day, but his driving was as aggressive as ever.

"So where are you taking me tonight Darling? You seem to be in a hurry to get me there. Promise me you'll go easy on me."

"Shut it bitch, we're going shooting."

"Just like old times. Our dates together are always so exciting."

"Now girls, behave yourself in the front seat there. No need to go all bitchy on us, this early in the day," said Sammy breaking his huffy silence.

"We arranged to go Clay pigeon shooting in Kells today. You knew that Mickey, didn't you?" said Gary.

"Yeah I was only teasing the boy racer here. I'd remembered. It's just that the whole set up reminded me of the old days when we would all go out together to discos at some barn in Kells. All dressed to impress and filled with the ridiculous expectation that we might find a girlfriend in a barn in Kells."

"Sure, that's where they kept all the best women in Kells. Locked up in a barn. Didn't you meet the wife in Kells, Gary?" teased Mark with a smile and Sammy joined in with a laugh that was louder than it needed to be.

"Fuck off!" Gary wasn't pleased.

Saturday 17ᵗʰ June 13.00

It had been my idea to go shooting on Saturday afternoon. I thought it would have stopped us from settling into a bar too early in the afternoon. Too much alcohol, too early in the day wouldn't have been a good idea, if we ever expected to last the pace long enough to go out for a decent meal in the evening.

But there wasn't much in the way of choice when it came to outdoor activities for four men no longer in their prime.

Gary had suggested a guided tour around the 'bad' parts of Belfast. A terror tour of West Belfast in a black taxi, with a driver who would no doubt have claimed to have fought for one paramilitary group or another and now made a little extra by telling a pack of exaggerated lies to gullible tourists wanting to hear about 'The Troubles', to gawk at the garish murals, and to have their photo taken in front of a peace wall. " …. and this is where I saw yer man shoot yer other man in cold blood one Friday night as I picked up a fare from the club down there. It was terrible, so it was. Living here in the Seventies, just trying to make an honest living while them'uns kept trying to kill us." I expect that no matter where you stepped into the taxi and who was telling you their story, it was pretty much the same story.

Shooting as a tourist activity in post ceasefire Northern Ireland, was no less ironic than being driven around to see the locations of a variety of mass killings. The country is full of guns. Legal and otherwise, and plenty of people are quite accomplished when it comes to using them. Legally and otherwise. The majority of Northern Ireland's Olympic medals have been won in the Shooting categories. Or in Boxing. Which makes sense now when I think about it.

I remembered that Gary was always fascinated by guns. When he was younger, he was always talking about guns and would regularly buy magazines like' Shooting Times' and 'The Field'. He even took to wearing a camouflaged jacket for a while until we pointed out to him that khaki green was the colour of choice for Paramilitary members on parade. A faded green parka jacket and a pair of oversized sunglasses were considered quite a fashion statement by our local paramilitaries towards the end of the Seventies. No self-respecting UDA leader would or wouldn't show their face without their gold rimmed Easyrider sunglasses and the obligatory big full mouth moustache, with just a hint of culturally inappropriate ginger hair. Some of them even wore little, short, khaki green jackets known as Bomber Jackets, just in case they forgot what they were supposed to be doing.

Gary stopped wearing his camouflaged jacket when he realised its significance, but I seem to remember Sammy and Mark continued to wear their little bomber jackets for at least another season. We were so fashionable in those days.

Clay pigeon shooting should be pretty tame. It wasn't as if any living thing was actually at risk of being shot. A few expensive rifles and a few cartridges fired under strict and expert supervision in the direction of an inert little flying disc. Tame but intriguing at the same time. I was looking forward to this aspect of the day. I expected that we all were.

The gun club seemed to be well established with many respectable members milling around, I suspected that many of them were ex-policemen or members of the various security forces that used to protect our homeland. There seemed to be quite a lot of them around for a Saturday afternoon. Shooting must be more popular than I'd thought. But very sociable in a strange way. It was a bit like the golf club but with more precision and purpose.

We were greeted by a man wearing a beige jacket with too many pockets, a carved wooden walking stick and an unusually firm handshake, obviously a NAPA, North Antrim Presbyterian Arsehole. It turned out that Sammy knew him and subsequently became the self-appointed leader of our little group of amateur snipers. We were led out to a long shed with one open side overlooking a wide-open landscape. There were others there already, shooting on their own and ignoring us. We were offered some jackets to wear by the man with the pockets who said that we might find the extra padding useful to protect our shoulders from the kickback of the rifles. But I noticed his jacket had more substantial shoulder padding than the tired and worn-out jackets he was offering to us. I felt mildly insulted and in a moment of pride and stupidity indicated that I would not be requiring his impoverished jacket. Gary and Sammy followed my lead and declined the tattered sleeveless low-vis vest.

Mark put one on, giving us all a swirl as he mocked the pointlessness of the unimpressive safety equipment.

"It suits you, it's a shame they didn't have one in your colour too." I said to the obvious annoyance of Mr Pockets.

"So, what else do we need? Some guns perhaps and some ammo too. What have you got?" said Mark.

"A lot of people bring their own guns, but I guess you guys didn't, so we will use some of the rifles we keep for visitors to the club and as for ammo, it depends on how long you're staying and how much you want to shoot."

"Just keep it coming until we hit something!" joked Mark, "We'll let you know."

"Ok some we'll do this two at a time. Could everyone put on these ear defenders. Please. This isn't optional and I assure you that you'll need them."

We shuffled towards the table to look at the rifles resting on the table. It had been a long time since I'd been this close to a gun.

"So, do any of you have any experience of guns?" asked Mr. Pockets.

I spoke first, declaring my novice status immediately, but there followed an awkward silence as the other three looked blankly at each other and then at the ground before eventually Mark spoke as if acting on everyone's behalf.

"Yeah, well some of us might have done a bit of shooting but it was a long time ago. Wasn't it lads?"

Saturday 17th June 13.30

Mark and Sammy went first. Gary seemed a bit reluctant and hadn't pushed himself forward. I wasn't in any particular rush to embarrass myself in front of those three.

"I thought you were really into guns when you were younger, Gary? You bought all the magazines and stuff."

"I suppose I did find them fascinating. Didn't every young boy? But that was before it became politically incorrect to run around your street holding a stick and making 'ack, ack' noises."

"Yeah but I can remember one night when we came out to a disco in some gun club in Kells and you were all excited when we found that unlocked gun cabinet."

Sammy and Mark, were already taking their turns with the guns. They lined themselves up and gave a nod when they felt sufficiently composed or sufficiently psychotic enough to fire. Mr Pockets would press something attached to a long wire and there would be a flurry of activity and pointing accompanied by a loud bang as the futile shot whizzed towards some piece of empty sky above the field where the clay pigeon had been just a moment before. Much cursing ensued which caused Mr Pockets to sigh in disapproval while at the same time smiling at the incompetence of his two novices.

"I thought you said you'd been shooting before?" I shouted over the noise.

"The guns were different back then and it's a lot harder than you think," shouted Sammy back at me.

The frequency of the shots was increasing, but the shooters were showing signs of frustration as the clay pigeons, appeared to be escaping unscathed.

"C'mon you two, give it a break and let us have a go." I suggested.

"I'm not giving up until I hit something" screeched Sammy, nodding furiously at Mr, Pockets.

"Well I need a break. My shoulder is starting to hurt. C'mon Sammy give Mickey and Gary a go."

Sammy straightened himself and the gun which he had now rested on the table in from of him. He glared over at Mark and snarled, "Whatever you say boss."

Without a further word, Gary had the butt of the rifle under his chin and had communicated to Mr. Pockets with the necessary nod of the head. One loud bang followed by a cracking sound. We all looked up to see the fragments of the clay fall to the ground in the mid distance.

"Again" accompanied by a nod.

Another bang, another crack.

I hadn't yet stepped forward or lifted the other rifle. It didn't seem to be the thing to do.

"Can we try two at a time".

"Ok, by me, if it's ok with your mates?" queried Mr. Pockets.

This time everyone looked in Mark's direction. He didn't even bother to speak. He just nodded firmly. It seemed to be what Mr. Pockets understood best. And in keeping with his preferred style of communication he just shrugged his shoulders and pumped his little handheld device twice releasing two clays from the distant trap and sending them to their almost instantaneous death. Gary was four for four and clearly motivated to do some more damage.

But Mark intervened, "Okay, you've shown us what you can do, there's no need to make us all look completely incompetent. Let Mickey have a go. Put down the gun and step away from the table, gringo."

"Nope, not this time. You don't get to tell when or what to shoot. Not now."

A short nod and Mr. Pockets rolled his eyes but complied. There were another two loud bangs but only one crack of clay. We all looked out to see one shattered clay fall to the ground while the other powered on and out of sight, still intact.

"I thought I'd let that one live" said Gary as he put down the gun and looked firmly at me. "Your turn."

Sammy looked at Mark. Mark looked at Sammy. As if one was expecting the other to say something. Something of substance. Something appropriate for the moment. Neither of them did.

I decided that maybe I needed to be the one who broke the silence. "So, it was more than just an interest in guns, Gary. You can actually shoot. You put those two other wide boys to shame."

"I always knew I could. We all knew I could. Didn't we, guys?"

I stood beside Gary and started to fire off a few single shots. After some near misses, I started to hit the occasional clay. Gary would dovetail beside me, continuing to fire while I reloaded. He didn't seem to be hitting as many of the clays now. Either he was trying to make me feel good or he had made his point earlier and had nothing more to prove.

We continued to shoot for another 30 minutes of so, alternating between the four of us, with ever increasing levels of success. Both Sammy and Mark improved enough to score a handful of direct hits and satisfy their original lust for glory. When they did manage to hit a clay, we would all kind of cheer together. When I say cheer, it was something more like an appreciative insult.

"Dead on, dickhead"

"Pretty straight eye for a queer guy"

"As easy as pissing a fly off a wall".

We would never have made it as BBC commentators covering the Olympics. But it was all good humoured.

Even Gary, seemed to have lost his anger and was even encouraging the other two. By the time Mr. Pockets decided that our time was up, and he had managed to squeeze enough money for extra cartridges and clays from us, everybody was smiling or laughing and boasting about their comparative success.

"Let Gary have one last go. Just to see what he can really do. Go on Gary. Try two clays from a standing start", taunted Mark.

"What do you mean by a 'standing start'?" I asked.

"Put the gun on the table and his arms by his side. One of us can shout 'pull' and Gary has to see if he can hit both clays".

"Whatever sirs would like", said a now exasperated and sarcastic Mr. Pockets. "But that's the last. We're done here."

Gary stepped forward deliberately not touching the gun, instead allowing Mr Pockets to insert the two fresh cartridges and lay the gun back down on the table in front of Gary.

"Just for old time sake, man." said Mark, in a genuine tone of encouragement.

"Show us how it's done." I said almost wanting to pat him on the back but realising that it might not be the best thing to do to a man bracing himself for an impending shoot out with some live ammo.

"Which one of you is going to call 'pull'?" asked Mr Pockets.

"You've done it before, Mark. Let me do it this time" suggested Sammy.

Gary didn't respond but shrugged his shoulders and flexed his arms, like an athlete before the start of a 100 metre sprint.

Mark nodded at Sammy and raised his eyebrows as if giving his blessing for the role he was permitting Sammy to perform.

"Give it both barrels, like we did for Angela. Pull!" snarled Sammy.

In one seamless motion, Gary raised the rifle from where it had been waiting on the table, slotted it under his chin and fired one single shot which created a small firework display by blasting the clay into a multitude of shattered pieces.

Instead of the second shot which we were all expecting, we stared at the sky as the other clay continued to fly over our heads. But Gary had already swung himself around and was pointing the rifle into Sammy's face. Less than a few feet away. Sammy froze. No one spoke. Mark straightened himself as if about to speak. Gary then swung the gun in the direction of Mark. Both rifle and Gary were pointing into Mark's face. Their gazes fixed for just a second but enough to stop Mark from continuing with whatever he had thought about doing. Gary moved the rifle slowly this time back to the rigid Sammy.

"Enough. I've told you before. Enough. I should have done this years ago."

"For God sake Gary ……"

Mr. Pockets, made his move. As if he had dealt with this kind of situation before, he stepped forward into Gary's line of sight and brought a single strike of his wooden walking stick downwards onto the barrel of the gun that Gary was still aiming at Sammy's head. This took Gary by surprise and broke his concentration, but the strength and accuracy of the old guy had been enough to force the gun out of Gary's control and onto the ground. Gary hadn't really tried to resist and seemed content to let the gun drop.

"I've had enough of you four. Get the fuck out of this club and don't ever think of coming back. Have you any idea how dangerous it is to mess around with guns like that. Get out. Now!"

He had a face that wasn't worth hitting.

"Ok, Ok, we're going." said Mark, taking a fifty pound note from his wallet and stuffing it into one of the many available pockets on the agitated beige jacket.

Gary had already started to walk away. Sammy stood still, not sure of what he should do next. I pulled him by the shoulder and pushed him forward in front of me, but close enough that I could pull him back if I needed to. My heart was racing but I felt I needed to take charge of the situation. "Mark, come on. Let's go!"

"I don't like it when people talk to me like that. Especially when I'm a paying customer. You old guys need to get over yourselves and stop playing with guns. This country doesn't need that shit anymore."

"Just get out. We don't need your sort here."

"Too right you don't. You've always had it pretty cosy. In your little private clubs."

We must have looked like a losing football team walking off the pitch. Heads down in a mixture of shame and embarrassment, as the last one to leave the pitch flicks two fingers at the referee.

Saturday 17th June 15.00

We had parked our car in the makeshift club car park on a cleared area inside the entrance gates and just beyond the so-called clubhouse. The clubhouse wasn't as grand as its members liked to think it was but if it was warm, secure and capable of serving cheap alcohol, it must have served their needs. I got the impression that we weren't going to be invited in to sample any of that cheap booze so like my three disgraced comrades I made my way, with Sammy in easy reach, to join Gary who was by now leaning against the car, in a casual but confident pose. It was only a short walk, but I was feeling quite breathless by the time I got to the car.

"Can you two please call a truce. I'm not enjoying this bickering and I'm not able for it."

"It was him. He started it!"

"For fuck sake, you just pointed a loaded gun in my face"

Just then Mark arrived behind us, "Now boys, you will have to behave yourselves or you'll both have to stay after school. Let's kiss and make up."

Neither Sammy nor Gary spoke, but Gary seemed less agitated than Sammy, who was very focused on every movement around him. As Gary pulled his hands out of his trouser pockets and reached out to pull open the rear door of the Merc, Sammy visibly jumped back as if to reach out to Mark as a human shield. Mark took control and pushed Sammy towards the front passenger seat, before walking around the car and taking the driving seat.

"Mickey, you sit on this side. I don't want that pyscho sitting behind me"

Gary just shrugged his shoulders and took the other back seat, "Be careful who you're calling a pyscho. It takes one to know one. Don't you think?"

Everyone took their seat and buckled up in silence. Sammy took a momentary look over his shoulder to check on Gary. Gary quietly stared out the window. Mark looked at Sammy like a mother threatening to scold a child. And I started to wonder what I could do to end the awkwardness.

Mark started the car and with his usual aggressive driving skills managed to kick up enough loose stones to not only engrave a large half-moon on the gun club car par but also leave a few stone chips on the sides of the adjacent cars. We were through the gateway and heading down the narrow country road before the dust settled and hopefully before Mr. Pockets or any of his fellow club members had the foresight to record Sammy's car registration number. They might be looking to make a claim on his insurance.

We continued for another five minutes with only the crunch of some bad-tempered gear changes to puncture the silence. All communication was now obviously on hold, no words were going to be spoken and no eye contact was going to be made. The best we could hope for was the occasional swear word from a frustrated driver more used to an automatic transmission, than the manual Mercedes he was now struggling to keep between the hedges.

I thought I'd try and improve the atmosphere.

"Guys I remember one night when we came out to another gun club in this part of town ……

"Yeah, it was when I was in the police and a member of a gun club near Kells", offered Sammy.

"I was the new guy in the local station and the gun club, but we came out here one night, to a barbecue and shooting match. I had been given free tickets and we were hoping to meet some girls. I think we had had a few drinks earlier on and things got a bit out of hand."

"Yeah, didn't we end up going home early or something?" added Mark. "You remember Gary, don't you?"

"Oh yes I remember it well." mumbled Gary.

I continued, "I seem to remember that Gary and Sammy started the evening chatting up the same girl. You were both trying to get into her knickers."

"At least one of us actually managed it." Interrupted Sammy.

Gary grunted and then said, "That girl became my wife "

I thought it best to move on, "So after a few beers in town, Sammy drove us out to the Barbeque, where we met my cousin who was there to take part in the shooting competition. I think he even had his own gun with him, and you were busy showing off another one you had found in the club gun cabinet. Didn't someone take exception to that? And that's why we were asked to leave early."

"Yeah, something like that." added Mark

"I think we were asked to leave because those two were still arguing over that woman" said Mark.

"She was a wee slut. She would ride you like a hobby-horse."

"She may have been a slut but she was my slut." pleaded Gary.

"Aye, a lot of people used to say that," teased Sammy.

I tried to calm things as we reached the edge of town. "I always thought Angela was a nice girl, who wore 'Stayfast' Presbyterian knickers. I don't understand why you would have done that Sammy."

"I pulled her just to prove that I could. And there wasn't anything he would have done about it." boasted Sammy.

Gary mumbled something, but none of us were able to make out what he was saying.

"You wouldn't like it if someone said something like that about your Jenny, now would you Sammy?"

"I was the only man, who ever got into her Presbyterian knickers, what she lacked in passion she made up for in loyalty."

"Aye, you could say that about a lot of people." snarled Gary.

We pulled into the car park at the hotel, and everyone bailed out, allowing the tension to dissipate into the summer air.

Sammy got back into the driver's seat. Gary stood seething with anger. Mark was already at the top of the steps waiting for the revolving glass doors to give him a chance to enter the hotel.

"Ok, so you only have an hour and a half to get your oxters freshened and a new shirt on. I've already booked a taxi to the Port. Be back here in reception by seven at the latest", but Sammy's car engine was already revving and drowning out my words. Gary was already crossing the road to the blonde filled car as his wife and two kids pulled up to collect him.

I headed up the stairs on my own. Mark had gone ahead, he clearly needed into his room as much as I needed into mine.

Saturday 17th June 18.00

The Adair Arms may only have 40 rooms, but there were enough for Mark and I to get one each on the same corridor. As I reached mine, I could see Mark was waiting by my door. He was doing his usual nonchalant pose. Leaning against the door pillar, like a drug dealer who was confident of not being arrested.

He was hushed but determined, "I just wanted to have a quick word with you about Sammy and Gary, before their little feud gets out of hand later tonight".

"Well it's not as if they are trying to hide their hostility to each other"

"It goes back a long way. To that night we were hunted from the Kell's Gun Club, in fact. Gary's wife Angela did the dirt with Sammy, at a time when she had just started dating Gary. She and Gary are very much the happy couple now, but Gary has never forgiven Sammy and Sammy hasn't got the wit to keep his mouth shut about it. Just another love triangle. Nothing unusual. Nothing to be concerned about. Who's to blame, well it depends on who's version you believe."

"Yeah, like many things it depends on which version you choose to believe, Gary does seem overly angry though."

I pushed past him and went on into my room. He didn't follow me, clearly content that he had said all he wanted to say. I wanted to shower, and I needed to make a couple of telephone calls.

I wanted to call my sister who still lived locally and confirm that I would visit her tomorrow afternoon. Then I made the necessary call back home.

"Yes, we had a good day at the Gun Club, and we've managed to stay off the beer all day. Tonight might be different story though. Honestly, I'm feeling fine, love. I'll ring you tomorrow. Love you too."

A shower, a new white shirt, a pair of Boss jeans, a fresh splash of aftershave and I was ready.

Choice of aftershave was important. You wanted to smell like a modern man but didn't want to smell like everyone else. As a teenager, you didn't want to smell like your mates either, so Brut and Denim were off limits, and you didn't want to smell like your dad, so Old Spice was to be avoided too. I decided on my usual Molton Brown.

Once downstairs, the smell of Denim was overpowering. Sammy had already arrived. Starting from the ground up, he was wearing shiny black brogues, black trousers that looked like the ones we wore to school, thick brown leather belt, white shirt, and faded blue denim jacket. What we used to call a Wrangler jacket and certainly not appropriate for a man his age, more like a drummer in a flute band.

Ballymena people are very musical and like many other ethnic tribes they have their own type of drum, called a Big Drum, purists prefer the Lambeg and the Bodhran, but never in the same place at the same time.

"I didn't realise it was fancy dress tonight. Is it a seventies theme or are you trying to look like one of the Undertones?"

"Fuck off! At least it still fits me. Don't tell me that you didn't keep your old Wrangler jacket."

"I didn't actually. Has Mark been down yet?"

Just then we heard the clump of the Cuban heals, as Mark arrived into the hotel lobby. He looked like a cowboy on his way to the local bordello. Complete with cowboy boots, skinny jeans and Hawaiian shirt. All that was missing was the sombrero, an accordion and the other members of the Mariachi band.

During the Peace Process, great steps were taken to de-commission the Accordion from Irish politics, in the past, both sides have been known to use these dangerous instruments to further their own agendas, and many have sustained serious injury as a result of an encounter with an illegally held accordion.

"Have you been on your holidays? Or did TK Maxx have a sale on?"

"Fuck off. At least I can carry it off."

"Do ya think?"

A car pulled up outside and dropped off Gary, with all the predictability of a slinky at the top of a staircase, in his tweed jacket and jeans, at least he fulfilled the agreed "smart/casual" dress code. I guess that's one benefit of having a wife.

"What's that smell?", we all spoke at once.

"Do they still sell that stuff, or is that the last of your Christmas gift set?"

"Fuck off!"

At least we all still spoke the same language.

Saturday 19th June 19.00

The taxi soon arrived, and we were on our way to the Port.

The Taxi had the smell of a new car, or so the little tree claimed, although I doubt if any of us really knew how a new car smelled.

As teenagers access to any car was a rare treat and the question of which school friend would be doing the driving on a Saturday night was always a big issue at school.

You only ever travelled to and from places with others from your own school, but you might occasionally talk to people from other Ballymena schools. Inter breeding among the different tribes was frowned upon.

Ballymena males have their own ideas about women. Or maybe it's the Ballymena females who have an opinion of themselves. For example, everywhere else in the world has hairdressers who cut hair, but in Ballymena only women who cut women's hair are hairdressers, men who cut men's hair are called barbers and women who cut men's hair are called "The girls who work in the barber's". Gender Equality was never popular in Ballymena. I once heard a local farmer say that he chose his wife because she had ample breasts and a delicious Victoria sponge. Women have their role in Ballymena and that's it. Women are either housewives or mothers. Always looking after their men folk, or eye candy with elaborate hairdos and expensive handbags. They are rarely sex slaves. Although you never know what goes on behind closed doors, especially on a Saturday night. Especially when there isn't anything good on the telly. I once referred to a friend's wife as "his partner", she never spoke to me again for years, she was so offended. "I'm his wife not his partner." So much for gender equality. And as for sex, well wasn't that the sole reason for having women around at all? We just marry the ones who let us play with their squidgy bits, as sound a reason as any for a sustainable marriage. As for younger women, they can easily tantalise Ballymena men, with their heavily pencilled eyebrows and look of surprise as well as their sexy knees exposed through the rip in their tight jeans. It has been often suggested that most of Ballymena's population was conceived in either Ken's car park in Harryville or the car park of Burberries Night Club in Portrush. It certainly explains the high number of cars with boxes of tissues on the rear parcel shelf.

But I do remember that my success rate with the local young ladies certainly did improve when my dad fixed up that old Mini, for me. I suddenly became a very popular designated driver.

"Do you remember, back in the day, our crowd going up to Portrush on a Saturday in that old scrap heap of a car you had?" chirped up Gary.

"I seem to remember that the old mini was very popular, with our crowd when going to Kelly's or anywhere else." I offered in my defence.

Mark was quick to divert the topic of conversation. "Do you remember big Eric Harvey who wore the gold corduroy trousers at school and was always wetting himself. He's a Councillor now"

"I remember one day he had a fountain pen in his trouser pocket when he wet himself and the ink spread down his leg like an impromptu chemistry experiment, all the rainbow colours of an oil slick." added Sammy.

"Do you also remember Miriam Kilpatrick from our class, no chest and knickers welded on with Rivets of Righteousness?"

"She wasn't the only one with knickers like that. I tried most of them over the years," said Mark, with a grin that was as much about his memories of old girlfriends, as it was about his success in diverting the conversation away from my driving duties.

"She never travelled to Portrush with us. She wasn't one of our crowd," said Sammy.

"She wasn't worth inviting, no tits and 'Stayfast' knickers" Mark confirmed.

"When I meet old school friends now, I always want to ask them if they ever managed to lose their virginity. Think of the fun you could have at a school reunion with that question?" said Sammy, "insufficient evidence of any Coves facing Donors."

"You never managed to get Ruth Burdock and her bumpy jumper to travel with us either, and I do remember you tried," said Gary.

"Oh yes, I tried. I remember that jumper very fondly. It was home knitted and not shop bought, so her bra or blouse were clearly visible when under pressure".

Sammy had a look of devilment in his eye, "Do you remember Angela, the one we called Car Park Kate."

I clumsily tried to deflect the obvious reference to Gary's wife, "That was hardly fair, Kate wasn't even her name."

But Sammy continued to twist the knife, "Well, I remember her very well, from the car park of the Toll Bar. She'd had a few, right enough, and was very accommodating. She even let me keep her knickers as a souvenir."

"Fuck up. That's my wife you're talking about. If you took advantage of her in a drunken state in a remote car park, that's less of a reflection on her than it is on you. She would tell a different story about that night. She says, she never gave you her knickers, but you took them,"

"Sounds like a dubious question of consent," added Mark.

"Back in the day, a ride was a ride. OK, we maybe weren't dating regularly, but she didn't fight me off either, so I don't think that I was in the wrong."

"For fuck sake, she was drunk and alone in a car park and you stole her knickers as some kind of trophy," said Gary almost crying.

"No, it wouldn't meet the legal standards of today, now would it, Sammy?" said Mark, as if he was so virtuous as to have never done anything similar himself.

"If you ever catch your wife sliding down the stair bannister, with no knickers on, it is reasonable to assume that she might have a dose of thrush," added Mark purely for information and based on personal experience, I expected.

Gary was clearly upset, "You have no idea, how difficult it was for Angela and I to come to terms with that shit."

"Don't be such a soft bugger. She kept her mouth shut, so should you. It was only a wee quickie in the car park." Sammy offered in his defence.

"You were a real bastard back in those days Sammy," I added.

"He still is, "Gary sobbed.

Mark gave me one of those looks that said, 'Let it lie, big lad'.

We continued north, along a very familiar country road. A road flanked on both sides by farm animals and grassland. Good farming country, if you were a wealthy protestant farmer. A straight but narrow road, like the people who lived near it. But a road where young drivers often went dangerously fast. Over the years many lives had been lost on that road, usually at the weekend when young revellers would have been returning home from the various pubs and clubs on the north coast. I had been fortunate to have driven up and down that road many times without incident, but then I was a good driver and known for it. I could be relied on, to get you safely to where you needed to be. My mind started to drift back to that night when I was needed to do some driving. I wanted to ask the boys about their memories of that night, but I wasn't sure if they would be willing to talk about it openly.

"Does anyone remember that night back in the seventies when I picked you guys up from the gun club in Kells and I drove you three out to Ahoghill?" I started to ask.

Firstly silence.

Then Mark calmly yet assertively announced. "I don't think this is the time or place for that discussion."

The taxi driver's face made it obvious that he knew that he hadn't been granted sufficient 'security clearance' to hear any more of that story. Silence resumed and we each concentrated on the view from our respective windows. Thankfully the taxi driver did the same. I'm not a good passenger in a car and prefer to do my own driving, especially on these roads.

I tried again to change the subject and relieve the awkward silence. "Does anyone remember David Gray's shoplifting exploits? He kept the whole school year supplied with Pop-a -Point pencils"

"Yes, and new golf balls too," added Gary. "I seem to remember he even stole a golf club once. A seven Iron, down his trouser leg."

Gary was making a brave attempt not to let his hurt show. Now for the first time, we could all openly understand the animosity between him and Sammy, it must have been hard knowing that one of your friends had known your wife before you did. A difficult pain to hide, for so many years. I felt for Gary now but I'm not so sure the other two shared my concern. Gary was a loyal friend, to us all, maybe not the life and soul of the party but loyal to the end. The kind of guy you could depend on to do whatever was needed to keep everyone happy and never to complain about being used. Angela and he were a strong couple. Apparently happy together since they first got together at school, two kids, a nice house and a nice new car every two years. They must have almost paid off the mortgage by now, and in Ballymena, that sort of thing is important. More important than great memories of distant travels or great parties. You were respected in Ballymena if you had a new car and kept it regularly cleaned.

The conversation may have lapsed to Mark's liking, but he took this as an opportunity to steer things his way again, he did like to take the driving seat.

"We were talking earlier about that night we were asked to leave the gun club disco. Do you remember the car Mickey," said Mark with a sheepish grin?

"I remember you said you had borrowed it but were very keen for me to do the driving", I replied.

Mark continued, "Yeah, I picked you up and we collected the other two before going for a few beers in town. The George, I think. The gun club disco was ok, but we were asked to leave because you and Sammy, were caught on, messing around with some policeman's gun. Then we all went home."

"Are you sure about that. Did we go straight home?" chipped in Sammy. "As I remember it, Gary was fascinated by that gun, but those policemen weren't so happy. There were very few women at that disco, that night."

"Always on the lookout for a shag, weren't you?" Gary responded behind a tight-lipped smile." I don't remember any of those policemen objecting to me having the gun. It was the club secretary who ordered us out. And I'm not sure we went straight home either."

"Of course, we did," insisted Mark. "We've talked about this before. It was just another good Saturday night spoiled by some over officious suits. Nothing more, nothing less."

"Ok, let's leave it for now." I decided to close this down and maybe check back later to find out if alcohol might shake up their memories and loosen their tongues. I had a feeling that the memory of that night was more of an implant than a real memory. I felt that I might have almost cleansed my memory of what really happened that night. It's easy to convince yourself that the story you tell is a better option than the truth. A case of, the best reason for telling a lie, is because you didn't want to tell the truth.

It took no more than 30 minutes to reach the outskirts of Portrush, largely due to the recent road upgrades of the Frosses Road. We would go straight down to the Harbour and get our name on the list, before catching a quick pre-dinner pint.

I said to the driver, "Can you drop us off at the Harbour first?" I think he was relieved to be allowed back into the conversation again.

"I can drop you off at the front of the restaurant, but I can't wait for you there, if you were wanting to go anywhere else."

"No, that'll be fine, thanks. We can manage from there and if we want to head out to one of the nightclubs in Kelly's or Magheraboy, we can always call another cab," I said.

"Well. Just remember, cabs aren't so easy to get in Portrush on a Saturday night."

"Oh, we'll manage," said Mark confidently.

Saturday 19th June 20.00

We got our names down on the list and a queue number for the restaurant, it was worse than getting wristbands for a Bruce Springsteen concert. Expecting a wait of maybe 60 minutes, we decided to visit the small front bar for some of the best served Guinness in the world, while we waited. There was a buzz about the place, and it wasn't worth travelling any further, just to have to return when our number was called to eat. The tiny bar was packed with men in polo shirts and brick red trousers along with trophy wives in unnatural blonde hairdos and enough animal print for a decent African safari.

As we made our way past the lone doorman, he seemed very interested in Mark but didn't bother to challenge us.

"Do you know him? Cos, I think he knows you." said Sammy.

"He's just doing his job, I suspect" replied Mark, but taking time for a good second look at the heavily built thuggish looking steroid junkie.

We squeezed our way into the tiny bar and ordered 4 pints of Guinness, we would enjoy them as we stood by the wall. There were no tables or chairs in this part of the bar, and we could admire the various pieces of golfing memorabilia on display on the walls. Although it was a harbour bar, it was favoured by many golfers. The Guinness tasted as good as it was reported to be, and other than the odd ostentatious gin, everyone was drinking Guinness and the bar staff were kept busy. I noticed that the burly doorman who had spoken to us on the way in, was still keeping an eye on us and was now talking into his mobile phone. Well, he was still keeping an eye on Mark, but hey, what's new. I mentioned this to the lads.

"I wonder what his problem is?" said Gary. "Should we go and speak to him?"

"I don't think it's ever a good idea, to speak to one of them sort. No point in bringing ourselves to his attention," said Sammy.

"Too late. He's coming over" I warned.

The doorman went directly to Mark, who was now fully aware of the developing situation. We couldn't hear what was said, but Mark took hold of the phone offered to him and began listening to someone on the other end of the line. His face suggested that he wasn't pleased, the confident grin had gone and there was even a suggestion of surprise in his eyes.

Just then our number was called to inform us that our table was ready. That was quick. We headed upstairs to eat. Much sooner than expected. On the way up, I took the opportunity to speak to the doorman.

"What was all that about?" I asked in a whisper.

"I recognised your friend, and I knew one of my friends would be interested to speak with him."

There was no time for any additional detail or discussion, the other three were already sitting down at the table which we had been offered.

I got the feeling that Mark was speaking for all three of them, when he questioned me as I re-joined them at the table. "Did you just talk to that piece of hired muscle?"

"I only wanted to know what that was all about downstairs, he only ...." I didn't get to finish my sentence.

"Ok! Ok! I'll tell you quickly before the food arrives." said Mark struggling to hide his frustration and maybe even a little panicked, "But then can we let it lie.?"

We pulled ourselves into a huddle, like schoolboys planning a prank, and Mark began his explanation "Ok, so it's no secret that I did a little bit of dealing before I moved to Spain. I may have left in a hurry without settling all of my debts. Hawkeye downstairs just sees himself as loyal debt collector and when he recognised me, he thought he might earn a few brownie points with the main men back in Belfast. The guy on the phone was the son of someone from Belfast that I might have known in the seventies. Don't panic, My bad. A simple enough misunderstanding, I'll get it sorted. Just enjoy your food and forget about it."

"You're still telling us to forget about things from the past, aren't you Mark, after all these years." I complained, "It's just like that night at the gun club, Mark says forget about it and that's what we do. Isn't that the way we do it Mark. 'Whatever you say, say nothing'. And no one will be any wiser."

The pressure on Mark was building and starting to show as sweat beads on his head just where his hair was starting to thin. He got up quickly and made his way to the bar, making the excuse that he was going to order a bottle of red wine for us. The more often you tell a lie, the more it resembles the truth. The food arrived. The steaks were good and exercised our mouths enough to allow Mark to recover his composure. But I wasn't going to let this lie. Now was the best chance I might ever have to get the closure that I had craved for most of my adult life.

"Why doesn't any of us accept the truth about that night. Will at least one of you guys just face the truth about the past. It's long enough ago now. It's history. It's in the past. It doesn't have to be a legacy. It can't hurt you anymore, unless you let it. I know it has given me many sleepless nights, but the past is a different place and you can't go there anymore. It happened, it's over, let it go. Face your demons and live the rest of your life. Unless you're waiting on death row. The mistakes you made in the past are in the past and shouldn't control your present nor determine your future, I remember that we didn't go straight home from the gun club that night. I drove you to Ahoghill. We took that gun with us and a man died." I was pleading.

Everyone looked at me, as if I was crazy. Sammy was the first to speak," Sssshhh. No one was ever charged for that killing. It's still an open case. It's a legacy issue. We could still be investigated by the Historical Inquiries Team. I don't need anyone knocking at my door and accusing me of collusion in an ancient sectarian murder."

Gary spoke next, "Sadly, I was the one that used the gun, but it was you and him that did the colluding".

Mark chose his moment to speak, "Would you three shut the fuck up? There was someone arrested for the killing of that shopkeeper and you should just let it lie. Like Mickey says. I know I don't need the past coming back to bite me in the ass, like that doorman thinks. Now keep your voices down for fuck sake."

"No, not again," I thought, "an ordinary catholic shopkeeper was shot at his front door that night. It was a sectarian murder of an innocent man condoned by people with easy access to police guns. Bad people, getting young lads to do their dirty work. We were manipulated and used; I've struggled with my guilt as the driver that night but I need to bring this to a conclusion."

The people at the next table had stopped eating and were staring at our table. Mark was glaring back at them with his most menacing stare. I was now staring at them too but sheepishly from a feeling of guilt. Naturally enough the other table chose to resume eating and pretend they hadn't heard what they knew they had heard.

There was plenty of silence, plenty of people preferring to say nothing for the sake of a quiet life.

After enough mouthfuls, Mark softly re-took control, "Anyway, wasn't there a guy involved in drug dealing arrested for that, we might have known him at the time, but I can't remember his name."

"Oh! You knew him alright; he was a big business rival of yours. You remembered his name well enough to give it to the police at the time.", snarled Sammy.

"The whole thing was a complete mess, but we didn't get caught, and I was only following orders anyway." whispered Gary.

"For fuck sake a man died, unnecessarily." I'd had enough, got up and went to the toilets.

I met the doorman again as I came out of the toilets. "Are you guys ready to leave? Do you need a taxi?"

I thought it might be a good idea to find a new location with a less strained atmosphere, and realising we had mostly finished eating, I decided it a good idea to follow up on the doorman's suggestion. I returned to the table and without sitting down, I announced to the guys that there was a taxi waiting for us outside.

Saturday 17th June 21.30

"Well that was quick," smirked Mark.

Outside we clambered into the waiting white Mercedes. Mark took the front seat.

"Good evening lads," grinned the taxi driver. " Where to? Good to see you again Mark."

Mark was surprised enough to pull his shoulders back into the seat and examine the taxi driver's face. "Do I know you?"

"Possibly not, but I know you, or more accurately, my mate's Da knew you. You met my mate the other night in Belfast".

"So that's who he was." stammered Mark.

"The Magheraboy please driver" I intervened. Why is it always my job to calm the situation?

"You'll not get into the nightclub at this time" said Gary.

"It's worth a try. We might know someone who could do us a favour." added Sammy.

That was always the way at Burberry's Nightclub, if you arrived late it would be a full house and the only way you could get in, was if you had a friend in the know or you bought a Pass Out ticket from the bouncers who ran a wee scam. It was a popular and successful place where people of both religions were able to mix in safety, knowing that no one cared what religion you were.

Gary spoke again, "No you won't get in, cos it closed a few years back, but Kelly's is still open, we could have a few drinks there for old time's sake."

The taxi driver obliged and dropped us off at the well-remembered entrance. We would only go to the bar, not into the huge nightclub.

"Don't worry guys, I'll see you later. Your return journey is already booked," shouted our taxi driver through his window as we bailed out and into the famous Kelly's Complex.

Kelly's was no longer just a disco with a bar, like it was in our day. It was a "Complex" now, which seemed to mean it had a labyrinth of rooms all decorated differently by some interior designer on drugs. We weren't there to dance, so we picked a room which had a number of little snugs and booths near the front of the original building. We chose one where we thought we would have some privacy and a clear view of the door. It's just an old tradition that people from Northern Ireland never like to sit with their back to the door. We also wanted enough quiet to be able to hear each other and not to be overheard by anyone else. It seems we were planning to do some talking.

There was no table service, so Sammy went to the bar and got four pints of beer. He didn't bother to ask anyone if they wanted beer or not, but at least he paid for them. I got the feeling that he knew we were settling in for a bit of a session and he was sure of getting his generosity repaid in future rounds. In Northern Ireland it is still considered polite to take turns to buy alcohol for everyone at your table. And to miss your turn and not repay the hospitality of your company was considered worse than farting in company. Many friendships and good nights out had been ruined by some tight arse not paying for his share of a night out. A freeloader would soon get a bad reputation for that sort of thing.

It was good to see that Sammy had finally learned how to behave in bars. We huddled into our booth,

The four of us sat on the two wooden benches on either side of a very rustic wooden table.

"Do you remember the old days in Kelly's? The White Pheasant lounge on a Sunday and the German beer on a Saturday night", began Mark with our 'Starter for Ten'.

"Wasn't that German beer just Pilsner?" replied Gary. "But it came in big bottles and made you look very cosmopolitan."

"Little wonder you found it difficult to get a woman, if you thought they were interested in the size of your beer bottle," teased Sammy.

"That's not what I meant, you twat. Anyway, I don't remember that many of them were queuing up to ride your pedals either," replied Gary.

"Now ladies, can we not just agree to keep this civil?" said Mark.

Just then three women cat-walked in, full of confidence and dressed to impress. They weren't teenagers looking for the disco and they didn't look like they were divorcees on the verge of Prosecco poisoning either.

We all paused to take a look and even enjoy the view. The women realised immediately that they had been noticed. Hair was swept back, breasts were thrust forward and their strides became longer and more precise, but they didn't agree on where those strides were going. Soon, realising that they were in the wrong place or at least in a place they hadn't intended to be, and making matters worse they were being watched, they variously stopped, turned and awkwardly bumped into each other.

Sammy reacted first "My head is in a spin, my feet don't touch the ground."

Gary continued," Because you're near to me, my head goes round and round"

Then Mark, "My knees are shaking baby, my heart it beats like a drum."

And finally, together in one voice "boum boum, boum boum"

"It feels like I'm in love", I said staring directly into the eyes of the leggy blonde woman looking back over at us. I suspected that her morals weren't as high as her heels.

She spun around as she fired back what she considered to be her best shot, "Good for you love, in your dreams, but I was hoping for something a bit younger, with more hair and less belly."

I dropped my stare into my beer. We all did.

The women left with their dignity and ours too.

Suddenly we didn't feel as young as we thought we were, even Mark's usual confidence appeared to wobble. Sammy was offended enough to fight back, "If you can't fight it or fuck it, then run away from it." Gary was his usual self and I was embarrassed.

Sammy was able to diplomatically break the mood "So now you've mentioned it, just how is your dodgy heart these days, Mickey?"

"Thanks for your concern, I feel fine," I replied, "I told you before, that I have this thing called Cardio Arrythmia or Atrial Fibrillation. Sometimes I have a rapid heartbeat which can cause some problems but as I said, you learn to live with it. I feel fine."

"Do you take a pill for it?"

"What would you know about pills? Sorry, I should have remembered, that you know quite a bit, eh, Mark?" teased Sammy. "I take a few tablets myself. For my diabetes."

"I take a regular Aspirin," added Gary.

"I could make some money out of you guys," concluded Mark. "That's enough Tablet Talk, that cheeky bitch has made me feel old enough without these Organ Recitals."

"It's best not to think too much about dying" I suggested hoping to close this discussion.

"Death is nothing more than the final stage of life. We're all going to die, not just today hopefully, the best you can hope for is to die in your sleep.

Death has more impact on the people you leave behind. So, deal with your demons, write your letters, let those that you love, know that you love them. And remember that you can't take it with you, so make sure you spend it all, doing the things you enjoy and with the people you love. You're only here once and not for very long. Life has no meaning other than the meaning you bring to it. Live an honest life and make the most of it. Noli Timere"

"So, says, the Reverend Doctor, Mickey O'Connor." sneered Mark.

"Did you never have any illnesses, that made you consider your own mortality?" I responded.

"Well, I did have to have a few Melanomas removed from my back a few years ago. The idea of skin cancer did scare me a bit, but I'm fine now." explained Mark.

"Too much sun, I'd guess, "injected Sammy, " I have diabetes."

"Type two?" said Gary.

"Yip, Type two and under control, so It doesn't get me a lot of sympathy." continued Sammy.

"Typical of us to get whatever lifestyle illnesses are available. I have Asthma, but that's not as trendy as it used to be." said Gary.

"While we're having this little Organ Recital, can I remind you that we are all old men, and we will all die sometime, so best get the beers in quickly" I concluded the dreary topic.

"Ask if they still do those big bottles of German beer and I'll have one of those," asked Gary.

"You'll be looking to get a request played by DJ Al -U-Minium, next. You can't get pregnant from listening to love songs", I replied as I headed to the bar to get another round in. We had hoped to get table service, but our discreet little corner was perhaps just a little too discreet to catch the bar staff's attention.

I excused myself as I squeezed past the group of ladies now sat at a nearby table unfortunately one of them looked as if when she was pregnant, she had cravings for chips and cream buns and her figure never forgot it. You would have had to turn her upside down to determine if she was a woman.

"Don't I know you? Didn't you used to be Mickey O'Connor?" announced the elegant blonde with the unnecessary amount of cleavage protruding over the top of her Karen Millen dress. I stopped to get a better look. The other three guys had noticed and were observing with more hope than expectation.

"I still am love, do I know you?"

"Yes, we'd often see you guys in the White Pheasant, back in the day. I think big Mark over there, even dated my sister here once." continued the blonde. "of course, none of us were blondes back then and I wouldn't actually describe a 'one-night stand' on a Saturday night in Kelly's as a date. There were no prior arrangements made nor 'follow up' proposed. I think Mark, was only really interested in getting what he wanted from the deal, as usual"

"I'll let him know you were asking for him." I suggested as I continued onwards to the bar.

"I wouldn't bother, but if it makes you happy." she mumbled, happy to have the last word.

At the bar, I ordered two pints of Guinness and two-pint bottles of Pilsner lager. I thought about getting the ladies a drink but didn't recognise the cocktail glasses filed with crushed ice and a pale pink liquid. "What are those ones drinking?" I asked the barman.

"From here it looks like paraffin, but I think it's a gin cocktail and could be expensive, "he snorted.

"I'll not bother then, I doubt if it would be a worthwhile investment," I replied before returning to our booth and planting the four drinks on the table. The four women watched me as I walked past.

Mark couldn't contain himself. "So, what were they saying?"

"I think they recognised you. I think the blonde one said that she dated you once."

"They're all fucking blonde! What is her name" shrieked Mark?

"I've no idea, Sheryl Crow, maybe."

"I never knew anyone called Sheryl Crow. Was she one of the Crows of Broughshane?"

"I've no idea, I was joking about the Sheryl Crow name. How would anyone ever remember all of the women, that you tackled? You would have chatted up a cracked plate." I countered. "In those days we wore our shirts outside our trousers so that she could wipe her hand and our DNA on our shirt tails.

"He wasn't the only one. Was he Gary?" sneered Sammy. "I managed to pull a few myself, back in the day."

"Managed! What the fuck does that mean?" snarled Gary. "Do you think you 'managed', my wife that night? Do you? I would doubt if a court would see it that way. I always suspected that maybe you spiked her drink that night before we went to the gun club, but then again, where would you have got the drugs", he paused and stared very deliberately at Mark.

"I thought we had agreed to let that one lie. No more mention of drugs or gun clubs," replied Mark.

"We didn't agree it. You just declared it, as always. Anyway, the only way Sammy boy ever got a woman, was if he picked up your leftovers or drugged them. Go on, tell us who your woman over there is?" said Gary.

"She looks a bit like Gillian, but the hair is different, or maybe Jennifer but I only remember her in a short little navy school skirt. Or if I picture it as a green skirt, then it could be Lorraine. She was the best looking woman who ever attended Cambridge House school." remembered Mark quietly, more for his own benefit than for ours.

The four women took intense interest in their paraffin cocktails, intent on not allowing us to know that they knew we were talking about them. But hair was tussled and tidied. Preening was in full flow. The glamour stakes needed to be raised. There could only be one winner and we were easily baited. Mark stood up and slid across to their table. We couldn't hear what he was saying but judging by the increased brightness in the room and the amount of tooth whitening treatments being displayed, I suspect that the four seats would need to be freshly wiped in the morning. He had the charm and the stature and the aftershave. He returned to our table with a confident grin and announced, "I still don't remember who she was, but she was cheeky enough to ask if I could get her any weed."

"Mark, everyone knew you were a dealer. Even the police knew. I never understood how you got away with it for so long." I said.

"Shut up, for fuck sake! Anyone could be listening." he snapped back, "You have no evidence to support that, I was never lifted. You had a cousin who almost got me into a lot of trouble once, saying stuff like that."

"Wasn't he the one who we met in the gun club that night and didn't he eventually get charged with that murder," I replied, while Sammy and Gary said nothing and looked at each other sheepishly.

"Look, I'm getting tired of this. Shut up, no more talk about that night please. I thought we had agreed not to mention this anymore when we met earlier this morning." said Mark, clearly getting angry and forgetting to maintain his winning smile for the four women, who were now starting to lose interest. They got up, knocked back the last of their drinks and left with a very deliberate and considered parting shot, "You suited those electric blue parallel trousers better than those skinny jeans you have on now."

"Ok, but I'd like to get a few details cleared up in my mind about what really did happen as opposed to what I believe happened." I pleaded.

We were ready to leave too but didn't want to look desperate by following the women out of the bar. We had seen the taxi pull up outside to wait for our departure and return to Ballymena.

As we walked out into the calm summer evening air, I was reminded of many nights in the past when we would queue at the little window to buy a bag of greasy chips before travelling home. The memory made me hungry, but I doubted, if my trend conscious pals, would share my craving for fat and carbohydrates. The car journey home would by-pass the fast food joints of Ballymoney and I was sure our old favourite burger bar, the SteerBurger in Ballymena, had long since closed. So, I opted for a visit to the mobile chip van parked up in the car park as the surest bet for a quick bite before the long drive back to Ballymena.

"You can't take anything to eat with you in the cab, mate," shouted the watching taxi driver.

"Save your heart the hassle." teased Sammy.

"I'll have a quick burger instead then. You can give me a couple of minutes to eat it, at least." I asked.

"Take as long as you like mate the meter is already running" retorted the driver "as long as you don't go for the Hawaiian burger, with the pineapple ring. That would just be wrong."

"What's wrong with pineapple?"

"It's a fruit, mate."

"Is that a homophobic statement or just anti-Hawaiian racism?"

"Fuck up. Eat up. And get in." said Mark.

Saturday 17th June 22.30

I quickly finished off my burger and got into the only vacant seat left in the taxi, the dreaded front passenger seat.

The front seat meant two things, mundane conversation with the driver about how busy he had been tonight and constant head turning to catch up on the backseat conversations. I didn't need to have worried.

"Hello guys, me again." said the driver immediately. "If you don't remember me, maybe you'll remember my Da."

"Aren't you the guy we met in Belfast last night?" I asked hesitantly.

"He is." said Mark.

"Hi Mark, we were hoping to have a few words with you, before you went back to Spain. I wish I could say my Da sends his love, but at least his old mates, have been asking for you," continued a smiling taxi driver.

"I'll just sit here in the middle then, so that I can hear what you have to say." replied a sheepish Mark.

This was going to be interesting, I thought, as I began to taste that burger in my mouth again along with the essence of the little swinging green tree. It was an obnoxious combination that cooked sickeningly in the dry air from the car heater vents flushing fully into my face.

"Could you turn down the heat a bit, mate".

"No problem. Does that suit all you guys in the back too? Eh Mark?"

"Yes please", said the three monkeys together.

Nothing more was said for a while as we drove out of the carpark onto the coast road, heading northwards to Ballymena. The full moon made it easy to pick out the greens and fairways of the Royal Portrush golf course between us and the sea. The course was looking well, as if ready for some big tournament or other. We turned off the coast road and travelled inland in silence. It was so quiet, that I almost wanted to ask the driver if he was going anywhere nice for his holidays. I resisted; I didn't want to distract him on the narrow twisting country roads.

We had driven past Ballymoney and were travelling in the direction of the famous Frosses Road before anyone spoke. The driver was picking his moment.

"So, Mark. About that money you owed my Da."

"I don't remember owing anyone anything," answered Mark.

"That's fine, maybe this will help you remember." He reached below his seat and pulled out an old Northern Bank coin bag. It was old and green and dirty and just big enough to cover the hand gun which he pulled from it. I didn't have to question how he came to have a Northern Bank bag.

I was expecting to have the gun waved or pointed in Mark's direction, but instead, Gary calmly reached forward, and said "Can I have a look at that?". The driver let Gary take the gun from him and continued to drive, without the slightest concern.

"I recognise this gun" said Gary, as he turned the gun over in his hands, examining it closely. "It's an old standard police issue Walther PPK pistol."

"Yes, it's the one that you lot used to murder that shopkeeper in Ahoghill."

"So it is!" exclaimed Gary as he rubbed the gun's barrel through his hands.

"Yes, it's been used very successfully over the years. It deserves a police pension for the service it gave to our cause over the years. But since it retired from the RUC, a few years back, during the decommissioning, it's ours now. Exclusively ours. We look after it. No more running to the officer who stored it at the gun club, to borrow it whenever it was needed. We did always ask permission before borrowing it though. Didn't we, Sammy?" said our taxi driver." Do you guys remember that night? I hope you do Mark, cos you might need to explain if this gun ever got handed in or into the wrong hands. You wouldn't want your old dealer pals, landing you in trouble, now would we Mark?"

"Are you threatening to inform the authorities, just because your Da never got paid all those years ago?" replied Mark. He clearly disliked the young man now for more than just his stupid haircut and his tattoos.

"Mark, you know the score. You have let a lot of people down. You owe them money. Is it any wonder they might say bad things about you," sneered the taxi driver.

Mark cleared his throat as he began his defence, "I had always paid my share back to the main men. That was the arrangement, as long as, I always kept to my own territory and gave them a percentage of what I made selling their drugs, I was allowed to do a little dealing to make myself a decent living. It suited everyone. It was a bit like a franchise agreement, like McDonalds or selling Avon. But I wasn't happy about the other aspects of the business. I didn't like guns, but I agreed to act as a co-ordinator. I agreed to organise a few special jobs, on the understanding that I couldn't be connected or linked with any crimes and could continue dealing on my little patch. But things got out of hand. People got greedy. I was given names and addresses of who needed to be taken out. Sometimes I knew the person, sometimes I didn't. There had been some suspicion that yer man might have been selling drugs too. He certainly had access to lots of tablets. I was told to get a team together, get a gun and go to a certain address in Ahoghill on a certain night. I was assured that there would be no proper investigation. I was assured that no one would ever come looking for me and certainly not forty years later."

"That would still have been the case if you had paid in our share of that last big deal, but you ran off to

Spain instead and then decided to come back to ponce around Belfast on a Stag Weekend."

I decided it was time to have my say, "I don't think any of us realised, how serious this was. Well, at least if I did, I tried to convince myself that it wasn't what I feared. I forced myself to believe that because I hadn't seen what happened, then I wasn't part of it. I just gave everyone a lift home that night. When we got to Ahoghill and stopped, I parked the car around the corner, intending to drive in the direction of Portglenone. I know I heard three shots, three muffled cracks, while Gary and Sammy were round the corner for a moment, but I never saw any gun and if it hadn't been for the sense of panic I saw, when you two got back into the car and the news I heard on the radio next morning, then I think I could still believe that you both had just got out to go for a pee. I wasn't being naive; I was turning a blind eye to protect my own sanity".

Saturday 17th June 23.00

We were halfway home and the silence in the car was crying out to be heard. The combination of a full moon and a cloudless summer sky was creating a strange light which allowed us a clear view of the rich North Antrim farmland on either side of the very straight new road. Protestant farmers had been blessed and rewarded with the best of the Northern Irish countryside to make the most of their family farms and maintain their wealth while other small farmers had made do with the poorer scrub hill land to the North East coast around Ballycastle. As we drove past, it seemed that even the many dairy cows in the fields were aware of the need to stand guard and protect their heritage. It seemed that every kind of animal was prepared to fight to keep things the way they were and out of the hands of them'uns.

Apparently Ballymena is bi-lingual. Many locals speak both English and Ulster Scots, which is a mythical language spoken mostly in late January and best described as bad grammar spoken with a Ballymena accent. In January it is often linked with Robbie Burns, the celebrated Scottish poet. If you ask nicely you can usually get a grant from the Ulster Scots people to celebrate a Burns night supper. All you need to do, is include Haggis on the menu and invite along a man in a skirt to talk jibberish. Irish is never spoken in Ballymena but can sometimes be whispered.

The car was beginning to feel like a confessional box, except crowded with friends who were judging your sins as much as the driver was acting as the priest taking the confession. But none of us would have seen things that way, as none of us had ever been in a confessional box. Even the smell of the inside of the car was starting to resemble stale Sunday clothes and the silence was still shouting guilt and pride as each of us tried to resolve our regrets. Gary kept turning the gun over and over on his lap. Sammy looked drunk and was drumming badly on the back of the seat in front of him, I was starting to feel sick and wanted the car journey to be over.

Sammy was struggling to contain his frustration and eventually began his confession. "I was only doing what I was told. I had provided guns before. Normally one of the usual guys would give me a gun and tell me to take it somewhere or give it to someone. You would always do what you were told by someone more senior in the lodge. I only actually used a gun once, at the beginning when I first went to the gun club. But after my first job, I didn't have to do any more shooting, I would just look after the guns."

Finally, Gary said his piece. "It was my first time, I felt I needed to impress everyone. I assumed you had all been through this before and now it was my turn to join the gang. I was angry that night. Angry about what Sammy had done. I just wanted to get it over and done with. I went with Sammy to the man's front door. Sammy said he knew which door it was. No one answered at first but when the guy did eventually open the door, we didn't speak. I fired three shots into him and he fell backwards into his hallway. I didn't see any blood but we didn't wait long enough to see or even to check if he was dead. I felt a need to pee and wanted to get back to the car as soon as possible. Sammy pulled the gun out of my hand before we turned the corner. Suddenly it was all over for me."

The silence had just got a whole lot louder.

Saturday 17th 23.00

The taxi had reached the outskirts of Ballymena and we were driving down the Ballymoney Road, when Gary started to make a call on his mobile phone. The four of us had walked home along that road many times together. A long walk home from the pub in the days when taking a taxi was considered too expensive. It was always a time for tall tales and drunken bravado.

Gary spoke into his phone, "We have just driven past the Countryman's Inn, we should be at the Adair Arms in about five minutes, so if you could pick me up in the car park, that would be great, Love. See you soon ...... I do too .... bye-bye, bye, bye."

The Taxi driver appeared to have lost interest, he'd heard all of the confessions now and seemed to have decided that our respective guilt complexes were scarier than any fear he could offer to manipulate us. Now that the secret was out in the open, it didn't hold the same threat anymore. Maybe it was time to write off that old drug debt, even though his father's mates were of that generation that rarely let go of anything. Old men from the seventies seemed happy to hold onto their old grievances forever and keep fighting the same old battles. He would try telling them to get over themselves. Again.

The taxi swung into the car park at the rear of the Adair Arms hotel. The car park was almost empty except for the silver Audi parked at an odd angle across a number of parking bays. The headlights shown directly on the slim figure of a blonde female leaning against the bonnet of the Audi. She was slight. Not tall but slim. Pretty and well groomed. Dressed in blue jeans and a white top. Her arms folded across her chest, drawing attention to her figure. She looked agitated possibly even angry or maybe just relieved. As the taxi's headlights moved across her shape, she didn't move.

The three of us in the back seat shuffled our bums out of the one door on Gary's side. We moved fast enough to ensure Mark would be left to pay the driver. The driver however didn't seem too worried about his fare, he turned and looked firmly at Sammy and said, "I'll see you soon, Sammy, make sure you look after that thing for me."

Mark was now standing by the passenger window and throwing another fifty-pound note at the driver. So that was all it took, fifty quid and a guilt trip. Mark was getting off easy,

The driver must have been satisfied with his payment and spun the car around, leaving us all looking in the direction of the silver Audi driver.

Sammy, staggered across and put his arm around her waist, pulling her into him as she straightened up, and swore at him.

"Get away from her", shouted Gary.

"Oh, he's very brave now, that little shooter of yours. But he's too frightened to do anything. Always was," countered Sammy, as he moved to one side, and gave the petite blonde the space she clearly wanted.

"Do ya think?" said Gary, raising the gun, which he was still holding. He pointed it at Sammy's groin, maybe only 12 feet in front of him. He squeezed the trigger with enough strength that his whole body seemed to be involved in the effort. There was a single bang and Sammy fell backward clutching his stomach as the blood soaked through his white shirt and onto his denim jacket. No one spoke or screamed, even Sammy didn't moan, but just writhed on the tarmac. Everyone's eyes told a different story, somewhere between fear and panic.

Mark calmly lifted his mobile phone to his ear, "Could you send an ambulance please".

Sammy stopped wriggling and passed out. So, did I.

Saturday 17th June 24.00

"There's been a shooting, we need at least one ambulance and maybe a police car", Mark was calmly speaking into his phone. Gary was now holding the blonde in his arms, her face buried in her hair and his neck. The gun dangled briefly in his left arm by his side, until Mark took it from him.

I was struggling to keep the lights apart. The dirty green and burgundy colours which were trying to merge together in my mind. I had no other sense or feeling. No pain. No fear. I was dying.

When the police arrived, they were greeted with a tranquil scene, a couple holding onto each other for dear life, two bodies and a man holding a gun.

Mark, quickly set the gun on the ground, and one of the policemen started speaking into his walkie talkie. The other policeman kicked the gun to the side and under the silver Audi, while holding his own pistol firmly in both hands and pointed in Mark's face.

"Get a grip." said Mark calmly, "These two need an ambulance, and I'm no threat to anyone."

"We only need one ambulance now. This guy has no pulse," said the policeman now kneeling over me, "We need paramedics for the guy who's been shot. And a private ambulance for the dead guy here, I don't know what happened to him."

The policeman continued to point his gun at Mark, just like he had been trained. Meanwhile the paramedics had arrived and started to work on the unconscious Sammy. I was on my way to the morgue in the private ambulance, which looked like an estate car with blackened rear windows. Gary's wife had decided that it was time to go home.

Across the road in Albert Place a light came on and a door was briefly opened to let a little dog out to shit on the street. The door closed again safe in the knowledge that tomorrow the occupants would go to church and drop their envelope in the collection plate as normal and all would be right with the world again.

"Let's get home love. When I die, I want to die first, so that we can be buried together, and you can be on top."

"In the movies, I would get one phone call. I'm too pretty to go to jail".

"Oooohhh".

I didn't say anything. I simply didn't exist any longer.

Sunday 18th June 15.00

The radio was on and 'Teenage Kicks' was playing on the Johnnie Walker Show. The Sunday papers were strewn across the coffee table as Gary and his wife held each other and their coffee cups tightly.

"We need to ring Mickey's fiancée, but I don't even know her name," said Gary.

"She'll be alright. Maybe a little sad for a few months, but ok, as long as she gets to keep the house" replied Angela.

"Is that all it takes? A few months and a pay out?" said Gary as he drew back and stared disbelievingly into his wife's eyes.

"It would work for me", she calmly replied, without realising how much she had just stung him and commenced the end of her marriage.

Now he knew how to stand up to manipulation and deceit.

Just then, before he could articulate a suitable response, the radio news announced, "and in Ballymena last night a man was arrested after a shooting in the town centre. One man was dead, while another received injuries which are not thought to be life threatening."

At Aldergrove International Airport, Mark was standing at the departure gate, as the police escort removed his handcuffs. "I don't know how you pulled off that one but get out of here and stay in Spain this time or you'll be arrested as soon as you set foot back in Northern Ireland," snarled the plain clothed senior police officer.

Mark smiled. He didn't feel the need to take a final look at the people watching and enjoying his departure. His Cuban heels echoed through the airport lounge as he was allowed to board first, while the queue of waiting Spanish holiday makers looked on and wondered who he was or who he thought he was.

Sammy sat upright in his hospital bed while his wife looked on anxiously from her bedside perch.

The ward was busy, every bed was filled with bald and over-weight men. There seemed to be a lot of young dark-skinned nurses rushing about but no doctors. The patients struggled to understand what the nurses were saying, since none of the men had ever bothered to learn any of the Filipino language, or any other languages in fact. Sammy tutted. He was heavily bandaged below his naked chest, and the various tubes attached to him suggested that they were the necessary ink to colour him back in from his unhealthy pallor.

"They didn't even give me the chance to choose the blood donor, this could be gay or even catholic blood that they're pumping into me, for all I know," complained Sammy.

"Does it matter?" questioned his wife," as long as we're going to be ok."

I lay in the morgue in Antrim Area hospital, which was quite defiant, as I simply didn't exist any longer.

On Albert Place, a man in a dark grey suit stepped out of his door and was annoyed to notice that there was dog shit on his door-step, but he managed to not tread in it.